Fast Gun Range

When Dan Tallow, a drifter, wins the deeds to a farm in a card game he thinks his troubles are over. However, arriving in the Montana valley where his new home will be, his sense of well-being is shattered when he has to step in to stop a lynching. His intervention makes an enemy of Mame Rockton, the valley's big rancher.

By involving himself in Rockton affairs, Tallow has made his first and only mistake: Mame has him framed for the murder of a US marshal who arrives to investigate the spate of Rockton crimes. Now she believes she can kill two birds with one stone.

Consequently the gallows seem to be Dan Tallow's certain end. But he has a determined ally in Hymie Goldberg, the young man he saved from being lynched, and a good friend in Reb Johnson, the woman whom he hopes to marry. Will all this and his own determination enable him to win through?

Fast Gun Range

Ben Coady

A Black Horse Western

ROBERT HALE · LONDON

© James O'Brien 2004
First published in Great Britain 2004

ISBN 0 7090 7598 7

Robert Hale Limited
Clerkenwell House
Clerkenwell Green
London EC1R 0HT

Typeset by
Derek Doyle & Associates, Liverpool.
Printed and bound in Great Britain by
Antony Rowe Limited, Wiltshire

CHAPTER ONE

Dan Tallow looked across the card table at the man sitting directly opposite him whose face, in stark contrast to Tallow's calm visage, was flushed and perspiring. The man's Adam's apple bobbed like a cork on choppy water. He glanced for the third time at the cards he held in his shaking right hand; three cards, two fours and a three.

The game was blackjack.

Tallow and the man called Seth Lowry were the only players left in the game. A pin dropping in the saloon would have had the report of thunder. Lowry brushed away the perspiration on his forehead to prevent it from dripping into his eyes, glowing with the frantic excitement of the addicted gambler.

'Fold, mister,' was Tallow's advice. 'Your luck's not in.'

Seth Lowry's greedy, whiskey-flushed eyes settled on the pot of one hundred dollars. Nothing like a poker pot, but the takings were sizeable for a game of blackjack in a one-horse burg.

Tallow had drifted into the game when another player had fallen out, having had no intention of playing cards when he had entered the saloon an hour before, though there was no denying his liking for blackjack; a liking that was sometimes downright irresistible.

He was riding a footloose trail, and had only stopped to slake his thirst and bunk down in the livery if the keeper could be persuaded. Otherwise it would be a night spent huddled in a doorway. Not such an uncommon occurrence for Dan Tallow. In Western parlance he would be called a drifter, a saddle-tramp, a trail bum, or simply a bum. However, he preferred to think of himself as a man searching for the right place to put down roots.

Dan Tallow had sounded a cautionary note when he had been invited to join the game.

'I've only got ten dollars. Hardly worth my while sitting in.'

A rangy man who had rancher written all over him had shoved out a chair. 'It's a slow night, stranger.'

Tallow had expected to be in and out of the game before his backside got warm on the chair. But an hour later he was still in the game, and looking at a stack of dollars in front of him. He was glad that he had not allowed his initial caution to prevail. A man with only ten dollars is a man who can think one of two ways. Lose it and tell himself when it was gone that ten dollars did not matter either way; or play safe and spend a sleepless night thinking of what might have been if he had risked it.

Folk said that blackjack, unlike poker, was a game of pure chance. Your luck was in or out. But that was not so. All games of chance were as much about reading faces and gestures as getting good cards, and Dan Tallow read faces and gestures well. His ability to do so had won him many pots. A couple of times it had saved his life.

'I think the dealer's right, mister,' was the rangy rancher's advice to Lowry.

The gambler's furtive eyes took in the men around the table. 'Stake me,' he begged. 'It'll be worth it.'

The reaction was negative.

'There's no chance of your luck changing tonight, Lowry,' the rancher opined. His gaze took in Seth Lowry's shabby clothes and gaunt face. 'Looks to me like your luck's been out for quite a spell.'

Lowry agonized. He glanced at his cards, seeing in his mind's eye a ten to match his two fours and a three. Making up his mind, his hand dived into his trouser pocket. He threw a parchment on the table.

'Deed to my property.' He assessed Tallow's

winnings. 'Worth a lot more than what you've got.'

Interest in what had been a mediocre game peaked. Men gathered round.

Tallow said: 'Be sensible. I'm not interested in taking your land, mister. Fold.'

'Not with these cards,' Lowry said adamantly.

Tallow repeated: 'Like I said, I'm not interested in taking your land.'

'You've got to honour my wager,' Lowry ranted. 'Ain't that so?' he asked the men at the table.

The rancher confirmed Seth Lowry's view.

Men crowded round the card table, rooting for Lowry. Tallow knew that if he declined Lowry's wager, at best he would be hauled outside and beaten senseless. And at worst, it being late at night and most of the men in the saloon liquored-up, he could be strung up. In Western towns, drifters were about as welcome as a rattler in a man's boot.

Tallow added all of his winnings to the pot.

'Card!' Lowry feverishly demanded.

Tallow slid the card across the table. Seth Lowry looked at it for a long while. Reaching for it and pulling back several times.

Tallow said: 'You can still fold, mister. You don't have to play.'

Seth Lowry seemed ready to accept Dan's proposition, but the intervention of a drunk standing behind Tallow put paid to that possibility.

'The bet's settled, mister.'

Tallow ignored the drunk. Trouble, he did not want. Because a man whose only possessions were a scarred saddle and a creaking nag was not a man who commanded respect. Perceived as a drifter, his stock with the town sheriff, unless the Crow Ridge badge-toter was an exceptionally fair-minded man, would be low. From past experience, his chances of coming out on the right side of any fracas would be slim to zero.

Risking the drunk's further displeasure, Dan Tallow repeated his offer to Lowry: 'Like I said, mister, you don't have to play this hand.'

Seth Lowry and Dan Tallow had a common bond. They were men down on their luck.

'I ain't no charity-case!' Lowry ranted.

He grabbed the card. King of Spades. Lowry's hand slapped the table. The saloon crackled with tension.

'Turn 'em, mister,' Lowry demanded of Tallow.

CHAPTER TWO

Tallow's hand hovered over his cards. He did not show his nerves. His grey eyes remained expressionless. No mean feat for a man whose heart was thumping with the beat of a war-drum. Seth Lowry's gloating was genuine. He was not bluffing. He held a winning hand.

Tallow reckoned that every cent he had was about to be snatched away.

Tough times were nothing new to Dan Tallow. Since the end of the war, like many other men rendered homeless and penniless, he had drifted from town to town and territory to territory. Chasing dreams, and always looking to greener pastures and El Dorado at the end of the next trail. Once or twice he had put down roots, and he had almost got married once. But soon the wanderlust returned and he was in the saddle again, searching anew for the silver lining that was supposed to be in every cloud. On a fool's search for a fool's dream.

His second worry was that whichever way the next couple of seconds panned out, he would still lose. Because the mood was running against him. No man wanted to see another man throw away the deed to his property, despite the foolishness of doing so on the turn of a card. And irrespective of how Seth Lowry had pushed Tallow into honouring the wager he had made, Dan's generosity of spirit would be forgotten in the outrage that would inevitably follow should he produce a winning hand.

'Turn the damn cards!' Lowry belligerently demanded.

Tallow turned his first card. Jack of Hearts.

Lowry took a sharp intake of breath, as did every other man. Every eye in the saloon was fixed on Dan Tallow's second card.

Dan turned his second card. Ace of Diamonds.

'That's luck I just can't believe!' Lowry growled.

Dan Tallow looked across the table at the stricken gambler.

'Are you calling me a cheat?'

The saloon hushed. Seth Lowry licked sand-dry lips. The only interruption to the cemetery stillness was the tick of the saloon clock marking time.

Lowry said croakily: 'I guess I am at that, mister.'

Tallow, tense as a bowstring, said: 'Take your

deed and let it be. I never wanted it in the first place.'

The other gamblers eased away from the table. The crowd separated.

'Mighty gen'rous,' Seth Lowry grumbled, 'seein' that you never won it fair and square anyway.'

'I won it fair and square,' Tallow asserted dourly.

'No good drifter,' someone in the crowd growled. 'Should be run outa town.'

Smarting, Tallow ignored the insult.

'Should be strung up,' another man said, his liquor-flushed face ugly.

Dan Tallow knew that there could be only one resolution to the impasse. Lowry, taking strength from the crowd's backing, began to think that he could reclaim his deed rather than accept Tallow's charity.

'The only way I'm takin' back my deed is when you admit your trickery,' Lowry said. 'Or. . . .'

Lowry kicked back his chair and stood up, his hand hovering over his sixgun.

The rancher at the table tried to act as an honest broker.

'Take the deed, Lowry,' he urged. 'No point in putting your life on the line, man.'

'Mind your own damn business, Ned Charles,' an unknown voice shouted from the crowd. 'Seth's got a right, if he thinks he's been cheated.'

'This,' Lowry chanted, 'is 'tween me and the drifter, and no one else.'

'Mister,' Tallow said in a hushed tone, 'I'll kill you. Don't want that to happen over a game of blackjack.'

Lowry settled his awkwardly worn pistol; a gun that was a working accessory rather than a killing tool. He had none of the gait that would mark him as a man who had a natural ability with a gun. Dan Tallow, on the other hand, did. Not that he had used his gun maliciously. Any shooting he had done had been solely for his own protection. But as far back as he could remember, he'd had a feeling for a gun, which he sometimes cursed and sometimes blessed, depending on the circumstances he found himself in. Now he was cursing. Seth Lowry was no hardcase. He was a desperate man who had fallen on hard times, fighting to hold on to his last smidgen of pride and respect.

Tallow's hope that he could avoid trouble went up in smoke when Seth Lowry dived for his gun. Before he could clear leather, Dan had him cold. Lowry stood stock-still under the threat of his gun. Dan returned the sixgun to its holster. He picked up the deed and handed it back to Lowry.

'This is over and done with, mister. Agreed?'

Relief flooding through him, Lowry nodded.

'Has this burg got a hotel?' Tallow enquired of the rancher.

'No. A couple of boarding-houses.'

'Recommend one?'

'Ma Barley's about the best there is. Her beds

have only thumb-sized bugs. Other houses have bugs so big they'd eat your ass off to the shanks by morning.'

'I guess Ma Barley's it is,' Tallow said.

'The house right at the south end of Main,' the rancher informed Tallow. 'Looks kind of crooked. It is, too. Andy Barley, rest his soul, built it. Never had a day sober in his life.'

Dan Tallow scooped up his winnings and left, his hand never far away from his gun. Trouble he was expecting, and he was surprised when he reached Ma Barley's without any.

The robust, florid-faced woman who opened the door to him announced: 'Ma Barley's the name. Two dollars for a bed. Three if you want breakfast.'

'And a bath. How much does that cost?' Dan asked.

'A dollar, unless you want me to scrub your back. That'll cost you two dollars.'

Tallow grinned. 'I think I can manage to scrub my own back, ma'am.'

'Want soap?'

'Doesn't it come with the bath?'

'Water comes with the bath. Soap costs extra.'

'How much extra?'

'A dollar.'

'Just as well I've had a good run of cards, ma'am,' Tallow observed.

'I'll set up a tub in the kitchen. Privy's out back. Supper?'

'I guess.'

'Two dollars.'

Tallow reckoned that Ma Barley would end up the territory's richest woman, if she was not already so.

'Won't be fancy,' she said.

'Supper or the tub?' Tallow asked sarcastically.

Ma Barley cackled. 'Both.' She stepped aside. 'Well, come in if you're coming, or else git.' She escorted Dan to a shoebox-sized room, wedged between the kitchen and the parlour. When she saw his gawping look, she explained: 'This room is for first-nighters.'

His curiosity piqued, Dan asked: 'Why is that, ma'am?'

'If they're trouble, or have unsocial habits such as breaking too much wind, they're nearer the front door and easier to toss out.' She cackled again. 'No refunds.' She held out her hand for Tallow's money. Then she went and examined the bowl of the oil-lamp. 'Oil's kinda low,' was her conclusion.

Dan already had a dollar in his mitt.

'Heck, the oil comes with the room.'

Relieved, Dan was about to pocket the bill when Ma Barley, smiling like a fox with a hen cornered, said: 'O' course, the wick costs.'

'Let me guess,' Dan said resignedly. 'A dollar?'

Ma Barley slapped her knee. 'You cotton on fast, mister. Will ya be staying a second night? If you

15

behave yerself, that is,' she cautioned.

Dan Tallow's smile was a wry one. 'I might, if I find a goldmine, ma'am.'

'Everyone calls me Ma. And if you're still here come tomorrow night, I'll move you upstairs where respectable folk sleep.' Before leaving, she reminded Tallow: 'Tub'll be ready in five minutes. Supper in ten. Ten more and you should have used the privy. Lights out then, if you have sense. Lamp wick costs.'

On his way back from the privy, Tallow met the trouble he had been expecting. Three men appeared out of the night, holding guns.

'Been expecting you fellas,' Tallow said.

'Then, in that case,' said the tallest of the three, and Dan recognized the voice of the drunk who had been prodding for trouble in the saloon, 'you'll know what we're here for.'

'We was plannin' on visitin' you anyway,' the second of the gun-toting trio sniggered. 'But we'll take your poke, too.'

'Not usual for a man to take his poke to the privy with him,' Dan said.

The leader of the group waved his gun for Tallow to lead the way.

Another figure stepped out of the shadows, brandishing a Greener.

'Drop 'em, gents,' he ordered.

The trio of robbers was astonished at this turn of events, and by who had initiated that turn. Dan

Tallow shared in their surprise.

'I griped a lot, but your win was a fair one,' Seth Lowry told Tallow. 'The stupidity was all mine.'

'Keep your nose outa this, Lowry,' the drunk warned.

'Yeah!' the second man snarled.

Lowry said: 'Be on your way. The man won fair and square.' Lowry held out the deed for Tallow to take.

'You're even more loco than I thought you were back in the saloon, you old fool!' the leader of the trio ranted.

'Git!' Seth Lowry ordered the men.

'OK. Keep your shirt on. And keep your finger steady on that Greener trigger, mister. Let's get outta here,' the drunk ordered his cohorts.

Lowry covered the men as they strode away, but neither he nor Tallow had counted on a fourth man in the shadows covering the robbers. His gun blasted. Lowry cried out and fell to his knees, his grasp on the shotgun slipping. The robbers did an about-turn and were joined by their crony. It was their cockiness in believing that Dan Tallow was done for that was their undoing. Tallow, with the swiftness of a mountain cat, threw himself into the darkness, grabbing the Greener on the way. Before the robbers could gather their wits, the shotgun exploded from the blackness and two of the quartet standing close together were blasted off their feet. The third man managed to cut loose with a

17

wild shot, before a pitchfork, which Ma Barley used in her vegetable patch, flew out of the darkness to embed itself in the shooter's chest.

The man who had shot Seth Lowry ran off in to the night and thought that he had got away scot-free until, from out of an alley, the figure of Dan Tallow loomed. The man was fast on the draw, but not fast enough. Tallow's gun exploded. The man was lifted off his feet and blasted through the window of the general store.

Men were by now piling out of the saloon. A lamp lit in the sheriff's office. Seconds later, a burly, grey-haired man in longjohns put in an appearance at the door, strapping on a gunbelt.

'Lowry's still alive,' one of the men from the saloon hollered, gently raising the gambler's head.

'Get him over to Doc Hanley's,' the sheriff ordered. His sixgun pointed at Tallow. 'Don't even twitch, mister,' he said in a no-nonsense fashion.

News of Tallow's would-be robbers was being called out.

'All dead,' was the verdict.

Tallow said: 'They tried to rob me, Sheriff. Lowry stepped in and caught lead.'

'That a fact?' The sheriff's voice reeked of derision. 'You're trying to tell me that Seth Lowry, who tangled with you, tried to save your hide?'

'That's the truth, Sheriff.'

'That remains to be seen,' the lawman said. 'Meantime, it's jail for you.'

'I didn't do anything to go to jail for,' Dan protested.

The sheriff tensed, expecting trouble.

'Like I said, that remains to be seen. Are you going to move towards the jail?'

'Don't have much choice,' Tallow said sourly. 'You're holding the gun.'

'A gun with a real touchy trigger to boot.'

Dan Tallow was turning in the jail door when a man called out from the doc's office.

'Sheriff, Seth Lowry's got some words to say to your prisoner.'

After a moment's consideration, the sheriff said: 'I guess we'd better hear those words, Tallow.'

Seth Lowry's eyes were rolling the way a man's do when he's hearing harps playing, and his breath, what little there was left, came from a long way off through tubes that were wheezing as they filled with blood, frothy globules of which were seeping through Lowry's purple lips.

Meeting Tallow's eyes, the medico shook his head.

Lowry beckoned the sheriff and Dan Tallow to him. His voice, a mere croak, made it necessary for both men to lean close to the dying man.

'Tallow did no wrong, Sheriff,' Lowry gasped. 'All the wrong was done to him.'

The sheriff nodded. 'If that's what you say, Lowry, it's good enough for me.'

Seth Lowry's shaking fingers fumbled in his vest

pocket. He withdrew from it the deed to his farm and shoved the parchment into Tallow's hand.

'That's your rightful property, mister. It's a piece of heaven needing the right owner, which I never was.' He grinned crookedly. 'Me having the wanderlust of all wanderlusts, and always wanting to see the next hand come good.'

He shuddered. His grasp on Tallow's hand tightened.

'Stop your wandering ways, son. Roots ain't so bad, once they settle in.'

Seth Lowry gave a sad whimper and lay still.

After a cursory examination, the doc declared: 'It's over.'

'You can ride out whenever you have a mind to,' the sheriff told Tallow.

Dan looked at the still form of Seth Lowry and said: 'I've got a friend to bury first, Sheriff, if that's OK with you.'

'Fine by me, Tallow.'

The day was a moody one. Heavy clouds pressed down on the cemetery. The tang of rain was in the wind. The plentiful growth of weeds and rough grass sighed as the fresh breeze rustled it.

'Lord, we ask you to judge our brother kindly,' the preacher intoned hollowly, 'and we ask that you take his soul in to your loving care for all eternity. Amen.'

The gravediggers lowered the coffin into the

grave just as the rain began to fall. The raindrops pattered on the coffin, and it sounded like Seth Lowry was asking to be let out.

Tallow was the only mourner. He stayed a while to pray. On his way down from the cemetery, he was approached by a man who wanted to purchase Lowry's deed.

'I'll pay a good price,' the man said.

Tallow answered: 'You haven't got enough money, mister. No one has.'

Upset by Dan Tallow's refusal to sell him the deed, the man became spiteful.

'You're a no-good drifter,' he griped. 'You'll lose that deed in the same way you got it. In some damn card game. Or you'll trade it for liquor or women.'

Dan did not engage the man further, seeing no point in fostering an argument. He had miles to travel. It was early summer. He hoped to make it to the Lowry place in time to make any necessary repairs before the winter set in. He expected to have to put right a lot of neglect.

His next stop was at the general store to replenish his war chest. Then he made his way to the livery to haggle over the price of a new nag. As he rode out of town, Ma Barley came to meet him with a hamper of coffee beans, bacon and blueberry pie.

'Free of charge,' she said.

'Are you sickening for something, Ma?' Dan joked.

21

'When you get where you're going, you write me, you hear?' she told Dan.

'I'll do better, Ma,' he promised. 'When the house is ready, you'll come visit.'

'You bet,' Ma Barley promised. 'And you find yourself a nice girl, Dan Tallow,' she called after him.

'Nice girls ain't half the fun, Ma,' he hollered back.

'Hah! See what mind you have for fun after a day behind a darn plough, young feller.'

As he rode away, Dan Tallow began to ponder on what the future might hold for him. Could he shirk his drifting ways? When a man had been foot-loose and sleeping under the stars for as long as he had, it would take something mighty special to have him quit his wanderlust. Dan wondered if the Lowry place had that magical something.

Only time would tell.

CHAPTER THREE

When Dan Tallow saw the valley where Lowry's holding was, he was at a loss to understand why or how Seth Lowry had ever left. He also knew that he would never again leave, except in a pine box. In his drifting days, now behind him he believed, Dan had seen a whole swathe of country, from the Yukon to the Mexican border, some of it bleak and stark with nothing to recommend it. However, he had also seen country that was lush, green and inviting. Many a time he had been of a mind to set down roots, but had for one reason or another not done so. But nothing he had seen compared with the valley he was now looking at. If a bit of heaven had been lost, this was where it had fallen. The glorious canvas of autumn was edging across the valley, breathtakingly beautiful in its diversity. Wild horses frolicked, jealous of the time left before the earth hardened with the first autumn frosts.

Dan had hoped to arrive earlier, but the need to

oddjob and earn a crust along the way had used up precious time. He had put together a poke of sorts. However, not knowing what his needs might be, it was difficult to know how far his savings would stretch. He had to be able to hold out long enough to get the farm in shape. He'd need workhorses, seed, implements, a good plough, winter supplies, all costing shekels. And once all the hard work was done, the winter had to be survived.

He could not discern the Lowry place from the map with the deed. Maybe he should now be thinking about the farm as the *Tallow* place. But Dan felt that he had no right to until he had made his mark. He hoped that it was to the south end of the valley, where the basin was protected by mountains and stands of pine that would act as a barrier from the winter storms, and in the growing season would offer their protection to the budding crops.

He did not know much about farming, only what he had learned working for a short spell for a dirt-poor farmer in Mississipi. But the winter would be long, and there would be little to do. That hiatus would give him the opportunity to learn. He knew that for the first couple of growing seasons he'd be lucky if he harvested enough of a crop to feed himself, with maybe a little left over to sell in the local town or to any ranchers around.

But he was not worried. He was home.

Dan Tallow's quietude was shattered by gunfire. The fickle wind blowing made it difficult for him to pin down its location. However, it took no time at all for him to spot its victim. A rider low in the saddle with four riders in hot pursuit, guns blasting.

Drawing rein, one of the riders exchanged his sixgun for a rifle. He took careful aim and fired. The fleeing man's horse stumbled and pitched forward. He fell heavily. The chase was over. Whooping exultantly, the riders charged to the stricken man. The rifleman, who was obviously the group's top dog, leaped from his horse and dragged the stunned man to his feet. He then dropped him again with a hammer-fisted blow to the side of the head. The other men joined in, kicking and punching their hapless victim.

Tallow's first reaction was to turn away and ride in the opposite direction. He was new to the valley, and it would be unwise to poke his nose in business that was none of his. It was, in Dan Tallow's opinion and experience, foolish to jump into a situation without knowing all the facts. It was a wisdom he had lived by; a wisdom which in the main had served him well. He would have turned away, if it had not been for the rope which one of the men slung over the branch of a nearby tree. He hated lynchings and lynchers.

Intervention was urgent. The rope was already round the man's neck. Tallow, wishing he had chosen another trail, reluctantly drew his rifle and fired in the air. The lynchers spun round, guns flashing in their hands. One of the men pointed to Tallow as the source of the interference. Dan approached, ready to engage the men should they choose to engage him.

They waited.

The leader of the men stepped forward, none too pleased. 'Who're you, mister?' he snarled. 'What're you doin' on Rockton range? And why're ya pokin' your nose in Rockton business?'

Tallow grinned. 'You're a fella who likes to get everything off his chest in one go, ain't you?'

A second man stepped forward. 'We got a rope that'll hang two as good as one, Spence,' he growled.

'Yeah,' a brutish, thick-necked hombre added. 'Shame to waste good rope on just one hangin'.'

The man called Spence snorted. 'You'd better talk fast, mister,' he warned Tallow. 'The boys have got their blood up, and don't take none too kindly to you spoilin' their sport.'

Tallow said: 'You fellas probably think that what happens here ain't none of my business—'

'That much you got right!' Thick-Neck interjected.

'And that's the way I figured, too—'

'If that's so, then what the heck are ya playin' at?' This time the interruption came from Spence.

Unfazed, Dan finished: '—right up to when I saw that dangling rope. You see, gents, I figure that a hanging comes only after a judge and jury says that there's to be a hanging,' he stated.

'That a fact?' Thick-Neck spat out a long spew of tobacco that streaked the toecap of Dan Tallow's boot. It was a provocation. Dan did not bite. The man was only looking for an excuse to kill him.

During the exchanges, a Mexican with the features of an Apache stood by with a sneer that would have a rattler slithering away in fear.

The hapless youngster who had been the gang's intended sport spoke for the first time. 'Thank you, sir,' he said to Tallow, in an accent that was a strange mixture of American and foreign parts.

The man called Spence kicked the young man's legs from under him, growling, 'Ain't no one gave you permission to open your mouth, Jew.'

'Damn rotten Jew!'

Thick-Neck kicked the youngster in the ribs. He curled up and moaned.

'Ride on, mister,' Spence advised Tallow.

'While you still can, *amigo*,' the Mexican added, unsheathing a hunting-knife. The sun reflected wickedly on the knife's blade.

'I was figuring on taking the youngster with me,' Tallow said.

'You'd share your saddle with a Jew?' Thick-Neck raged. 'What kinda toerag are ya?'

'The kind who will shove this rifle up your ass and pull the trigger,' Dan Tallow said with quiet menace.

Untroubled by Tallow's threat, Thick-Neck scoffed, 'Yeah?'

'You can count on it,' Tallow said.

Sensing a formidable opponent in Tallow, Spence decided on a less confrontational approach to resolving the impasse.

'The Jew's been sniffin' round Beth Rockton. That would be Mame Rockton's daughter.'

'Stepdaughter,' Thick-Neck corrected.

'Same thing!' Spence barked, not appreciating the interruption. He considered Tallow. 'You prob'ly don't know, you bein' a stranger an' all, but Mame Rockton owns most of this valley, and what she don't own, don't make no difference anyhow. Now, would you like it if a stinkin' Jew was sniffin' round your kid, mister?'

'Depends, I guess.'

'On what?'

'On whether he was invited to sniff or not.'

'Are you sayin' that Beth Rockton's hot for a Jew?' Spence asked in awe.

'Can't say,' was Dan Tallow's reasonable response. 'Don't know the facts of the matter, do I?'

'You don't need no facts to understand that no Jew comes near a woman round here,' Thick-Neck snarled. 'Except their own filthy kind.'

Tallow asked: 'Did the boy do any wrong to this Beth Rockton?'

'Never got close 'nuff,' was Spence's reply.

'So, what *did* he do?' Tallow enquired. 'Other than being a Jew, that is.'

The men exchanged puzzled glances.

'You don't get it, do ya?' Spence said. 'Round here bein' a Pole or Irish is bad 'nuff.' His look was glacial. 'But being a Jew is more than 'nuff!'

'Figured so,' Dan said.

'I think we got us a Jew-lover here, fellas,' Thick-Neck grunted.

'No Jew has ever done me wrong,' Tallow said. 'And even if he had, I don't figure that I'd string him up simply for being a Jew.'

'Ain't you been listenin' to a word we've said?' Spence asked Tallow. 'The Jew's been sniffin' round Beth Rockton.'

'I heard,' Tallow drawled. 'And if he's done nothing but sniff, then he ain't broken no law that I know of. Why don't we all agree that the boy's got his punishment and has learned his lesson, and just ride away?'

'We're not goin' anywhere until the Jew swings,' Spence said, his face flushed.

'You're hanging him just because he's a Jew,' Tallow said quietly.

'Good enough reason, I figure.'

'I don't,' Tallow said, in an even quiter tone. 'In my book, a man's got a right to his beliefs.'

'Told you he was a stinking Jew-lover, Spence,' Thick-Neck snarled. 'Let's hang them both.' His mean eyes fixed on Dan Tallow. 'Him first.'

Tallow's boot shot out and poleaxed Thick-Neck as he attempted to haul him from his saddle. Stunned by Dan's audacious reaction, the others backed off under the threat of his rifle and looked to Spence for a lead, obviously hoping for an end to the fracas. Their relief was palpable when Spence, like them, backed off.

'Get Ike in his saddle, Rico,' he ordered. The half-breed helped Thick-Neck on board his horse. 'The Jew is all yours,' Spence told Dan, but added chillingly: 'For now, that is.'

Rifle at the ready, Dan Tallow watched them ride away. The Jewish boy was pinching himself, still not able to grasp that he had truly escaped a lynch-rope.

'Do you know where the old Lowry place is?' Dan enquired of him.

'Yes.'

'Well, mount up and take me there. I've got a farm to get ready.'

'Farmer? You?'

'Don't know if I like your tone,' Dan said.

'Seth Lowry hire you?'

'You ask a lot of questions, boy,' Tallow barked, 'for a fella who's just cheated death.' He took Lowry's deed from his pocket. 'I'm the new owner.'

They were riding for some time before the younger man said: 'Do you know the kind of trouble you've brought on your head, mister?'

30

'No. Not exactly. But,' Dan Tallow sighed, 'I'm sure that I'll soon find out.'

The young man was shaking his head fit to come off.

'Not because you saved my neck,' he said. 'Sure that will bring trouble, but—'

'But what?'

'The real trouble will come because you plan on settling in this valley. There's no way that Mame Rockton will stand for that.'

'Don't figure on trouble from a woman,' Dan said.

The other man laughed, but with no humour.

'Mame Rockton wears a skirt all right, but she's not a woman like you know a woman, mister. If the devil's taken human form, he's hiding inside Mame Rockton for sure.'

He shook his head and rolled his eyes.

'I guess you've had trouble of a kind before, mister. But you really don't know what trouble is, until you have to deal with Rockton trouble!'

CHAPTER FOUR

'How do you figure on trouble?' Dan Tallow asked the young Jew. 'I've got clear title. Everything is legal and proper.'

The young man laughed bitterly and scoffed.

' 'Cause Mame Rockton considers that every blade of grass in this valley is Rockton grass. Every tree is a Rockton tree. Every drop of water is Rockton water. You think that a piece of paper is going to let you walk into this valley, Rockton territory, and put down roots? Hah!'

'Don't see why not?' Tallow said. 'It happens.'

'Yeah. Some place else, it happens. Not in Rockton country, mister. If they were ready to hang me for handing a wildflower through the sitting-room window to Beth, what do you think Mame Rockton will do to you for wanting to put down roots here?'

'A darn woman rancher,' Tallow pondered. 'Ain't natural, I say.'

'That about describes Mame Rockton all right.

And don't you think that she ain't as tough as any man you'd care to tangle with. She's had more men hanged than you've got fingers to count on.'

Tallow snorted. 'Kind of stupid dallying with wildflowers with such a witch around, wasn't it?'

'I'm in love with Beth Rockton, body and soul,' the young man declared. 'And she's in love with me, and that's a fact. She told me so,' he said emphatically, when Dan Tallow raised a doubting eyebrow. 'She is, an' all!'

'What's your name, boy?' Tallow enquired.

'Hymie. Hymie Goldberg. Why d'ya want to know?'

'We've got to put something on your tombstone, don't we?'

'Tombstone!' he exclaimed. 'I ain't got no plans to put on wings, mister.'

'Yeah,' Tallow drawled. 'That's what I figure you'll be doing, if you try and deliver any more flowers to Beth Rockton.'

'I ain't going to stay away,' he said with youthful determination.

'They'll hang you for sure the next time,' Tallow warned the young man.

'Not if you're around, they won't. Never saw no one put legs under Spence Barrett before, like you did.' He cut loose with a wild laugh and slapped his knee. 'He wanted to kill you, for sure. But he was as scared as a hen with a prowling fox in the neighbourhood.'

'I won't be,' Dan Tallow said. 'Around, I mean.'

'You're still going to settle in the valley, ain't you?'

'Sure am.'

'Well, that means that you'll be around. Any trouble with Spence Barrett and I'll tell him that you'll be calling on him.'

'Hymie,' Tallow barked, 'what happened back there when I got your scrawny neck out of a noose is only going to happen once. Count on it. Now, my advice is to stop mooning over Beth Rockton and hightail it out of the territory, while you still can.'

'Kind of ornery critter, ain't you?'

Dan Tallow was beginning to regret having saved the youngster's neck.

'You'll need help to put the Lowry place to rights,' Hymie said. 'I might look like a sapling, but I've got the strength of an oak.'

'Very poetic,' Tallow said, deadpan. 'But I've got all the time in the world to put the Lowry – no, dammit,' he corrected, 'the *Tallow* place to rights.'

'That your name?'

'Yes. Dan Tallow.'

'Well, Dan,' Hymie Goldberg said, full of a cocky confidence he had no right to have after the close shave he had just had with disaster, 'how about hiring me?'

'Can't.'

'Why not?'

'Don't have any spare cash. That's why not.'

Hymie Goldberg's dark eyebrows furrowed, but it took only a second or two for his infectious optimism to reassert itself.

'You can owe me, Dan,' he said.

'Ain't it usual for a whippersnapper like you to call an elder Mr?'

'Yeah, I guess. But I can't go round calling my partner Mr now, can I?'

Astonished, Tallow yelped, '*Partner?*'

'Sure thing, Dan. In no time at all we'll have,' he pointed, 'the Tallow place in order.'

Tallow's jaw dropped on seeing the desolation of the former Lowry farm. The cabin, which was barely standing, was passable compared to the rest of the place. The barns had completely collapsed and lay in rotting mounds of debris. The yard was completely overgrown. The farm machinery, or what used to be farm machinery, was either busted or rusted. The fields spreading out from the ramshackle mess had obviously lain fallow for many years. Even with a miracle, Dan Tallow could not see how the place would ever again function as a farm.

'Ain't pretty, is it?' Hymie said.

'Ain't anything,' Tallow replied.

'Well, what did you expect? The place has been rotting for as long as I can remember.' Dan looked at the arm round his shoulders. 'But don't you worry, Dan. We'll have this place looking spick and span in no time at all, partner.'

Tallow could not believe his misfortune. A rotting farm and a loco boy. It was, he concluded, more misfortune than a man deserved.

CHAPTER FIVE

'Blackjack,' Dan Tallow said two days later, in answer to Hymie Goldberg's question about the provision of supplies.

'Blackjack?' Hymie repeated, doubtfully.

'Have you got another way to make fast money, Hymie?'

'No, sir. But you said that you had a poke of sorts.'

'Ain't going to be enough for our needs.' Dan went into the dank back room of the cabin. A minute later he came back with a fistful of dollar bills. 'It's blackjack, Hymie.'

Hymie Goldberg obviously had his doubts about the wisdom of gambling as a path to security.

'What if you lose, Dan?' he asked.

'I won't, Hymie.'

'That's what the last owner of this farm said,' Hymie reminded him.

The pathetic sight which Seth Lowry had been,

winged its way back to Tallow's memory. But he reminded himself that he did not have the kind of card sickness that Lowry had had. His approach to gambling was sensible, Dan told himself. Until he looked at the much-needed dollars he was about to risk.

'I won't lose, Hymie,' he said. He walked purposefully to the cabin door. He turned to say goodbye to find Hymie dogging his heels. 'And where do you think you're going?'

'To town, with you.'

'Oh, no, you ain't. I need to be able to concentrate on playing cards. With the poke I've got, if I blink I'm out of the game. So you stay put. I don't want to have to worry about you.'

Dan had not gone far when he turned in his saddle to ask: 'In which direction is town, anyway?'

'Well, it's kind of difficult to explain, Dan,' Hymie said, scratching his dark head, mischief animating his brown eyes. 'But if I was on the road now, I'm sure that I could find the way.'

'Hymie Goldberg,' Tallow said, 'you're way too smart for your own good.'

Grinning from ear to ear, Hymie rode up alongside Dan Tallow.

'Ready, partner?' he asked cockily.

Willow Creek took most of an hour to reach. When they finally did reach it, Dan Tallow reckoned that it had not been worth the effort. It was postage-stamp small. Its citizens looked righteous. The church, standing on a rise, looked down on the town like a brooding judge.

'You sure they even play cards in this burg?' Tallow enquired of Hymie Goldberg.

'Well, the town's got a whole pile of religion,' Hymie informed Tallow, 'but the Tipperary Shamrock saloon is a bit of hell in paradise. It's where the crews from the big outfits in these parts spend their hard-earned dollars, dancing, drinking, whoring and playing cards.'

'How come it ain't been burned down?' Tallow wanted to know.

'Well, that's because a couple of the church Elders are secret partners in the saloon with Daniel Murphy. He's the Irishman who owns the Tipperary Shamrock.'

'Ain't that kind of hypocritical, Hymie, church Elders reaping the profits from sin?'

'Darn, it's business, Dan. What's business got to do with religion?'

'Hah!' Tallow scoffed. 'Everything, when hypocrites masquerade as holy men.'

'Hold on there now,' Hymie Goldberg protested. 'You'll have my head spinning with that kind of smart guff, Dan.'

'How come, you being a Jew from foreign parts, you talk such good American?' Tallow asked.

'Used to work in the Tipperary Shamrock. Then one day Mame Rockton rode into town and told

Murphy to fire me or lose Rockton trade.'

'Mame Rockton doesn't like you very much, does she, Hymie?'

Hymie's face grew long and sad.

'She's not the only one. I'm a Jew, Dan. No one round here likes Jews.'

'How come you are around here, Hymie?' Tallow enquired.

'A pure mistake. My folks busted a wagon wheel and came into town to have it repaired. Someone overheard my father praying. Hanged him there and then. Ma took poorly and died two days later. I was ten years old.'

'How did you survive?'

'There was an old Indian living in the valley. He took me in. Dead now, too.' He laughed sadly. 'Shot in cold blood 'cause he was an Indian.'

'What have you got to be to survive round here?' Tallow asked.

'Real lucky for a start,' Hymie Goldberg answered simply. 'And not be an Indian or a Jew. Irish, too, maybe.'

'You know, Hymie,' Tallow said, 'maybe Seth Lowry didn't do me any favours after all, lumbering me with the damn deed to his property. Maybe I should just sell up and move on.'

'Move on?' Hymie yelped. 'You don't look like no quitter to me.'

'Ain't a matter of quitting, Hymie,' Tallow barked. 'It's a matter of good sense, and knowing when you're beaten.'

'You know what,' Hymie groused, 'it's a darn shame that of all the *hombres* who could have got their mitts on Lowry's deed, it had to be a whiner like you!'

'*Whiner*?' Tallow yelled.

Hymie leaned sideways in his saddle to come face to face with Dan.

'What else?' he said. 'Quit if you like, but I'm staying put.'

He rode ahead, contemptuous of Tallow.

Dan's first urge was to yank the youngster out of his saddle and thrash him for his impudence. But as his anger eased, he realized the truth of what Hymie Goldberg had said. He was doing what he had been doing since the end of the war, quitting. Always finding a reason to go around instead of facing up to his problems. And now he was doing it again. It would be a whole lot easier to saddle up and ride on instead of getting to grips with putting the farm right. For the first time he saw himself as others saw him – a saddle-bum.

'Hymie,' he called out.

'You still here?' Hymie called back, not bothering to turn in his saddle.

'You're hired.'

'Yeah?' Hymie said, disinterested. 'For how long? Until your feet get itchy?'

Tallow spurred his horse and drew level with Hymie Goldberg. He grabbed his reins and drew him up short.

'I'm staying put, Hymie.'

Hymie studied Dan's face, and then smiled.

'You know what?' he concluded. 'I think you just might have put down roots at that, Dan Tallow.'

'Now that that's settled, Hymie, blackjack. And after that, we'll knock up the general store for supplies.'

'That's if the cards run your way,' Hymie said. 'And if you're still sucking air after your visit to the Tipperary Shamrock,' Hymie added, sombrely.

CHAPTER SIX

Stepping inside the Tipperary Shamrock, Dan Tallow instantly realized, was akin to stepping into a nest of vipers. It surprised him that, in a church-dominated community, the saloon had such a size-able clientele bellied up to the bar. Scattered about the place were a couple of card games, and from one dark corner came the skittish giggle of a saloon dove.

'You are a bold one, Francey Collins,' the dove said, and flesh slapped on flesh.

'Dang it!' came a male voice from the shady corner. 'Ain't I just given you five dollars, girl?'

'Sure you did, Francey,' the saloon dove cooed. 'But you've just taken ten dollars' worth of liberty, honey.'

'All I've got is three dollars more,' Francey complained.

There was the rustle of paper being exchanged, and more giggles.

Hymie Goldberg, hogging Tallow's heels, stared, his eyes trying to penetrate the dark corner.

Tallow said: 'Go mind the horses, Hymie. You're too young for this devils' den.'

'Young? I worked here, remember? Swamped it out every day.'

'Are you going to argue about everything I tell you to do?'

Hymie groused, 'OK, I'll mind the damn nags.'

'And don't curse,' Tallow rebuked him.

'What's your poison, mister?' the burly barkeep enquired of Tallow.

'Whiskey.'

'That's Murphy,' Hymie muttered in a croaky aside, pointing to a man as Irish as bacon and cabbage dealing cards at one of the tables. 'Stay clear of him, Dan. His deck's got at least ten aces.'

Red-faced and mean-eyed, Tallow reckoned that crossing Daniel Murphy would be as foolish a venture as kissing a rattler.

'See those rope-marks round his neck?' Hymie murmured. 'The English tried to hang him.'

'Tried, Hymie?'

'Yes.'

Wide-eyed, Hymie continued: 'But just as the gallows trap-door opened, a man dressed all in black, riding a black stallion, cut the rope with a single shot. He then hoisted Murphy on his back and fled with him. The man's eyes glowed like a wild beast's, and smoke puffed from his nostrils. It

44

was the devil on horseback. Murphy escaped and came to America.'

Dan grinned. 'The devil, huh?'

'With the devil on his side, folk don't upset him, Dan. You steer clear of him, too.'

Sizing up Daniel Murphy, Tallow reckoned that the proprietor of the Tipperary Shamrock had himself, with Irish guile and cunning, circulated the yarn about him and the devil being buddies. That way no one would give him any trouble. As for the rope-marks round his neck. . . .

'Has Murphy always lived in Willow Creek, Hymie?'

'No. A gambler passing through town once, said that he knew Murphy in Dodge.'

And it was in Dodge that Tallow figured some-one had tried to hang the Irishman.

'Maybe the devil came to America with Murphy and got inside Mame Rockton?' Tallow wryly suggested.

Hymie's eyes lit up.

'Wouldn't surprise me none, Dan,' was his verdict.

'Go and mind the nags, Hymie,' Dan said.

'We've got two kinds o' whiskey,' the barkeep told Tallow. 'One that'll rust your kidneys, and one that will kiss 'em. The kissin' variety costs. Which'll it be?'

'I'll settle for a beer,' Tallow said.

'Beer it is. If you want a glass to drink it from,

it'll be fifty cents extra.'

'A bottle will do just fine.'

Tallow paid. He turned from the bar to give his attention to the card games in progress, and found Spence Barrett, the Rockton foreman, standing behind him.

'Well, now, folks,' Barrett sneered, 'this here is the Jew-lover me and the boys was talkin' 'bout.'

'I don't want trouble,' Dan said with a quiet resolve. 'I've come to play cards, that's all.'

A man looking out the window said: 'The Jew's right outside, Spence. Maybe we should finish what was in'trupted earlier?'

Barrett sneered. 'You're just chock-full of good ideas, Randy. But maybe this gent wouldn't like that?'

The man at the window made a show of shivering in his boots. A howl of laughter went up.

'Like I said,' Tallow retorted, when the jeering stopped, 'I've just come to play cards.'

'Does that mean you don't mind if we string up the Jew?' another of Barrett's cronies taunted Tallow.

Uncompromising in his attitude to lynchings, Dan Tallow stated as much.

Catching sight of a man creeping up on him, knife at the ready, Tallow spun around and smashed the beer bottle he was drinking from across the creeper's head, opening up a deep gash that gushed blood. Dazed, the man staggered back.

Tallow felt the prod of a gun in his back.

Spence Barrett said, 'A couple of you fellas hold him.' He addressed the injured man. 'Ace, you take your revenge. All you want of it.'

Dan fought against the two beefy wranglers who pinned his arms behind his back, but it was a futile struggle. The man called Ace rained blows on him. Obviously his intention was to beat him to death. No one intervened. Dan's legs were wobbling when Hymie Goldberg filled the batwings, toting a rifle.

'Leave him be!' he commanded. 'You fellas back off,' he ordered the men holding Tallow.

Spence Barrett chuckled. 'Well, if it ain't the Jew boy. You know from which end of the gun the bullets come from, Jew?' He strolled menacingly towards Hymie. 'You're going to hang, Jew. Right now.'

A splinter of wood spun up off the floor and lodged in Spence Barrett's left leg from Hymie's shot. Howling, the Rockton foreman danced around the saloon. A whiskey bottle on the bartop near the man who had been laying into Tallow, shattered in a thousand fragments as Hymie cut loose again. A sliver of glass cut a furrow through Ace's right cheek, rocking him back on his heels.

'Dan,' Hymie called, 'can you make it over here?'

Tallow said, 'Just about, I reckon. But first. . . .'

Tallow swung a haymaker at Ace. He heard the

47

satisfying snap of the man's jaw. Ace spun wildly out of control and went straight through the saloon window. Tallow drew his sixgun and covered the saloon's patrons as he limped out of the bar.

'You look like a horse stepped on your dial, Dan,' Hymie observed.

'And that's what it darn well feels like too,' Dan Tallow replied, through mushed lips.

As they backed out of the saloon, Ace was struggling drunkenly to his feet in the street outside. Tallow put him back down on the flat of his back with a boot to the side of the head. Spence Barrett was still howling inside the saloon.

'Think we'd best make fast tracks now, Dan,' Hymie urged.

'Hymie,' Dan said, screwing up his puffed eyes to look at their horses at the hitch rail, 'which one of those twelve nags is mine?'

Hymie Goldberg held the saloon under the threat of the Winchester while Tallow struggled to board his horse, every bone in his body aching. He cut loose with a volley of shots into the saloon, and then scampered to his own horse. As they raced along Main, men burst from the Tipperary Shamrock, guns blasting. But luckily for Dan Tallow and Hymie Goldberg, anger made their aim wild.

'Where did you learn to shoot like that, Hymie?' Tallow asked.

'Beginner's luck, Dan,' Hymie said. 'First time I fired a rifle.'

Dan Tallow glanced back at the men vaulting into their saddles to give chase.

'Beginner's luck, huh?' he groaned. 'Great, Hymie. That's just downright dandy!'

CHAPTER SEVEN

Tallow's horse and the winded nag which Hymie Goldberg was riding, were no match for the oat-fed mounts on which the Rockton crew were in pursuit. The breeze of their bullets was getting uncomfortably close. The sizeable gap that their sprint had opened up was closing by the second.

'I think we've got a problem, Dan,' was Hymie's opinion.

To which Tallow responded, deadpan, 'You don't say, Hymie?'

A bullet whipped Tallow's hat from his head and spun it in the air. If the bullet had been a fraction lower, the ragged hole in the hat's crown would have been in his skull.

'Got to get lower in the saddle, Dan,' Hymie advised.

'My damn chin is already resting on my saddle horn,' Tallow flung back. 'Why the hell didn't I let

you hang? If I had, I wouldn't be riding helter-skel-
ter with my ass in the air and my head coming
round to meet it!'

'We've got to switch trails, Dan,' Hymie said.
And glancing behind him at their charging
pursuers, he added: 'Fast!'

'That a fact, Hymie?' Dan said, in a tone as dry
as Mojave sand. 'Got any ideas?'

'The left fork up ahead leads to Deadman's
Canyon.'

'How appropriate,' Tallow growled.

'We can make a stand there.'

'A stand, you say? There must be a dozen men
on our tail. Is that the best idea you've got?' Dan
grumbled.

'It's one more than *you*'ve got,' Hymie retorted,
cheekily.

A shotgun blasted. The branch of a tree crashed
on to the trail, making it necessary for Hymie to
take evasive action. For a terrifying second, both
horses brushed together and almost went down.
Tallow's horsemanship won the day, and saved the
fleeing duo from a disastrous and probably fatal
end to their flight.

'You know what, Dan?'

'What, Hymie?'

'It ain't fitting to be running scared like this.'

'You figure, huh?'

'I figure. Jews have been running scared for too
long,' Hymie said defiantly, slowing his pace.

'What've you got in mind, Hymie?' Tallow asked urgently, and with no small degree of trepidation.

Hymie Goldberg's defiance strengthened.

'I figure it's time to take a stand against tyranny and bigotry,' he spunkily declared. 'To stop running scared. To stand and be counted, Dan!'

Tallow grabbed Hymie's reins and dragged his slowing horse along.

'Save the speech for when you've become a United States senator, Hymie. Right now, our necks are only a breath away from a rope. We can think about fine ideals once we've saved our necks.'

A bullet buzzed close enough to Hymie's face to shave him.

'You know, Dan,' he said, urgently, 'you might have a point at that.'

He raced ahead of Tallow, cutting sharply to the trail that led to Deadman's Canyon. Tallow, a stranger to the country, was left with no choice but to bring his horse's muzzle as close to the tail of Hymie Goldberg's horse as he possibly could.

Jubilant, in the certainty of nailing their quarry, the Rockton crew had taken to a wild yelling and chanting that would have scared the living daylights out of any war party of Indians.

Drawing level with Hymie, Tallow asked: 'You know this Deadman's Canyon well, Hymie?' Dan's unease shot sky high when he saw the shifty look in Hymie Goldberg's eyes. 'Hymie, you damn critter,' he growled.

'It'll be OK, Dan,' Hymie said, in an upbeat fashion that did nothing to reassure Tallow. 'I've got beginner's luck, ain't I?'

'Holy shit!' Tallow swore, as Hymie veered into a canyon that looked about as dead-ended as a corpse's future. 'Is there a way out of this?' he queried urgently.

Hymie's lack of response might, Tallow thought, be down to his headlong dash. But he figured that that was a mighty big maybe. And as they galloped deeper into the canyon, the trail getting narrower and narrower just like a trail does when it's going nowhere, it did not surprise Dan Tallow any when it petered out into a small basin with nothing but solid rock ahead.

'I think maybe we should have veered right a while back, Dan,' Hymie said.

Fearing Tallow's wrath, he added hopefully: 'At least there's no trees to hang us from.'

Tallow said grimly, 'Hymie, it's likely that we're not going to be around for much longer. But if by any chance we get out of this, I'll damn well string you up myself!'

The pursuing horses were slowing. Spence Barrett and his cronies obviously knew now that there was no hurry, and they could savour the entrapment of Tallow and Goldberg.

'Best do what we can,' Tallow said, resigned to the fact that any resistance would be token.

He'd been looking to put down roots; now it looked like he would be planted. The most permanent roots of all.

CHAPTER EIGHT

'I'll take the rifle,' Tallow told Hymie. 'You do what you can with this.'

Tallow handed over his sixgun, acutely conscious of its half-empty chamber and his greatly depleted gunbelt. Bullets cost money, and he had had a difficult enough time making the long journey to the valley without, as he saw it, wasting good dollars on bullets he would probably never need. The same went for the Winchester. His box of shells was almost empty.

'Try and make every bullet count twice,' was Dan's forlorn advice to Hymie Goldberg.

The horses stopped in their tracks, and there was the shuffle of boots through the rocks just beyond the final twist in the trail that led to nowhere. Spence Barrett, wily as a mountain cat Tallow reckoned, would draw their fire and wear them down, which would not take long. Hymie's sixgun exploded nervously at nothing more than a hat held aloft on a stick. There was no comeback from the bullet, which meant that Hymie's shot had hit air and nothing more. Tallow held his temper in check, seeing no point in making his last moments in Hymie Goldberg's company acrimonious.

A double rifle volley bit the dust near Tallow, close enough to let him know that the shots had come from an ace marksman who could have just as easily dispatched him to wherever he was bound for. The same shooter had Hymie dancing a jig a second later. Mocking laughter echoed through the canyon.

'Hey, Spence,' a man called out, probably the shooter, 'did you know that Jew boys can dance?'

More laughter.

'Tell ya what, stranger,' Tallow recognized Barrett's voice, 'if you want you can walk outa here, but you leave the Jew behind.'

Hymie Goldberg went as pale as new milk. It was a deal that a man facing certain death could not refuse. He glanced at Dan Tallow, trying to gauge his reaction to Barrett's offer.

'It's a deal that you've no right to expect, mister,' Barrett sang out. 'Grab it while you can, I say.'

'He's right, Dan,' Hymie said, in a voice that was a mere croak. 'You go. You don't owe me nothing.'

Dan Tallow would be lying to himself if he said that the temptation to accept Spence Barrett's offer was almost impossible to resist. He was thirty-five years old, with lots of good years to come, especially if he got the farm in shape. It was downright evil that now, when he had something to gain, after years of shiftless wandering, he should have to face the kind of decision that went with the predicament he had landed himself in.

'Go on, Dan,' Hymie urged Tallow. 'I guess as a Jew I never stood much of a chance in this country anyway.'

Tallow made his decision.

'You've got a right to live like any other man, Hymie. Besides,' he said with a grin, 'I figure that in time to come, the Jews and the Irish will own America.'

He called out to Spence Barrett: 'Thanks for the offer, Barrett, but I still don't hold with persecution and lynchings.'

'You're a fool, mister. Time to flush 'em out, boys,' he shouted. 'But remember,' his voice was hard with bigotry, 'I want the Jew alive.'

A fusillade of gunfire coming from every direction rained down on Dan Tallow and Hymie Goldberg, pinning them down without any hope of returning even the modest reply they could make.

A second's break in the hail of lead gave Tallow a chance to return token fire. A man climbing higher to have a duckshoot angle on Dan and Hymie yelped, grabbed his side, missed his footing and toppled down through the boulders. When his toppling came to an end, Tallow was pleased by the man's moans and groans. His sole concern now would be counting the number of broken bones he had.

'Ned,' Spence Barrett yelled. 'You OK?'

The man's response was more moans and groans.

'You bastard,' another man called out. 'I figure we should hang him with the Jew, Spence.'

'I ain't stoppin' ya, Larry,' Barrett called back.

'So, let's go get the bastard!' Larry shouted.

An even greater hail of lead followed, intended to pin Dan and Hymie down rather than kill them. Shameful hanging would be their lot.

CHAPTER NINE

Then another gun opened up, its bullets going towards Barrett and his cronies. Tallow looked behind him to a figure at the highest point of Deadman's Canyon. The sun was in his eyes, but there was no mistaking the figure of a woman. And even in his present danger, Tallow could appreciate the shooter's shapely silhouette. Lead continued to be delivered with unerring accuracy, and it was time for Spence Barrett and his cohorts to dance and duck.

'Time to be getting on home, boys,' the woman called out.

'Hey, Mrs Johnson, ma'am!' Hymie joyously hailed the woman. 'Did you know that American cowboys can dance?'

'This ain't over, Jew,' the Rockton foreman promised, and extended his threat to include Dan Tallow. 'Or for you either, interloper.' Then he turned his attention to the shooter. 'Mrs Rockton won't take kindly to your interference in Rockton business, ma'am.'

A volley of shots sent Barrett and his cohorts scrambling for their horses. The Widder Johnson's bullets bit at their heels as they fled the canyon.

'Who the hell is that?' Dan enquired of Hymie Goldberg.

'That, Dan, is the Widder Johnson. A woman fit and shapely enough to drive any man loco with wanting.'

That was a fact that Dan Tallow had already ascertained.

'Thank you, Mrs Johnson, ma'am,' Hymie hollered.

'Hymie Goldberg,' the Widder Johnson called back, 'why haven't you finished painting my barn?'

'Well, I've been kind of busy saving my hide, ma'am,' was Hymie's answer. 'And I've been helping your new neighbour.'

'New neighbour?' the Widder asked.

'Stand up,' Hymie instructed Tallow. 'Meet Dan Tallow, Mrs Johnson. The new owner of the Lowry place. Take a bow, Dan.'

Dan, to his incredulation, curtsied.

'A real mannerly cuss, ain't he, Mrs Johnson?' Hymie laughed.

'The Lowry farm, you say?' the Widder Johnson quizzed.

'Yes, ma'am,' Dan confirmed. 'Something wrong with that?'

Reb Johnson, a clever play on the name Rebecca, she being a Virginian by birth and a Southerner by conviction, replied with untypical bluntness for a Dixie belle.

'Yes, I reckon, is the answer to your question, Mr Tallow. You see, you're the latest in a long line of hole-in-the-head gents who thought they owned the Lowry place.'

'I don't understand, ma'am,' Dan said, conscious of a great big hole opening up to swallow him. 'I've got the deed to prove my claim.'

Even though she was some distance away, there was no mistaking Reb Johnson's scepticism.

'Won it in a game of blackjack, did you?'

'Yes,' Dan replied.

The yawning hole suddenly got bigger.

'Seth Lowry's gambled that deed a thousand times in a thousand games. But none of those parchments were legal. Copies, Mr Tallow. That's what they were. Seth had a whole bunch of them printed from the original deed, on parchment that would fool a lawyer.'

Dan's mind raced back to the night that Seth Lowry had given him the deed. Would a dying man, facing his Maker, lie?

'Got the deed on you?' Reb Johnson asked. 'I'll know if yours is the genuine article or not the second I set eyes on it.'

'It's back at the cabin, ma'am.'

'Then let's go see. But don't get your hopes up,

Mr Tallow. My guess is that it's just another copy, not worth the parchment it's written on.'

On the journey back to the farm, Dan managed to shake himself free of his dour thoughts long enough to thank the Widder Johnson for her help and neighbourliness.

'Hymie and me were as close to being harp-players as made no difference, ma'am,' he said.

She chuckled. 'Think nothing of it, Mr Tallow. I kind of like to get an opportunity to lay lead on Rockton scum. How did you and Hymie get yourself in such a fix anyway?'

Hymie answered. 'Spence Barrett and his hardcases were about to hang me when Dan stepped in to thwart them, Mrs Johnson. Then Dan reckoned that he'd go to town to play blackjack and—'

'Don't approve of gambling,' Reb Johnson rapped.

'I figured that it was a way to get enough money for supplies,' Dan explained, strangely anxious not to earn Reb Johnson's disapproval.

Reb gave no quarter on her views.

'Gambling's not the way,' she rebuked, sternly.

'The Rockton crew were in town and took up where they had left off, Mrs Johnson,' Hymie said. 'That's how Dan and me ended up in Deadman's Canyon in a fix.'

'If you go looking for the devil, you'll find him,' Reb opined. She screwed up her blue eyes against the sun, which was highlighting the tint of red in her golden hair. 'What were they hanging Hymie for?' she enquired, of Dan.

'Well, Hymie is sweet on Beth Rockton,' Dan explained. 'And Hymie says that she's sweet on him, too. But when all's said and done, being a Jew was the main reason for hanging him.'

'Ain't surprising,' was Reb Johnson's observation. 'Jews around here are about as popular and as welcome as a snake in your bed.' She glanced sideways at Dan Tallow. 'You like Jews, Mr Tallow?'

'It ain't a matter of liking or disliking in my book, ma'am,' he said. 'I reckon that no one's got a right to hang a man because of his beliefs.'

'Mighty high-faluting principles,' Reb Johnson chirped. 'My husband, the late Jack Johnson, figured like you do.' She sighed a world-weary sigh. 'Before he was shot in the back for his high-minded ideals,' she concluded bitterly.

'And you reckon that it was Rockton hardcases who did the shooting?' Tallow prompted.

'Usually, round these parts, any rottenness can be traced back to Mame Rockton. If Satan's got kin, then I reckon Mame Rockton's his sister.'

They rode on in silence for a spell, until Reb Johnson said: 'Ask the question that's bothering you, Mr Tallow.'

'That'll be Dan, ma'am.'

'Then ask your question, Dan.'

'OK. Are your views the same as the late Mr Johnson's?'

Reb Johnson drew rein and studied Tallow.

'I've got nothing against any man or woman of any colour or creed,' she stated, but qualified: 'Except if your monicker happens to be Mame Rockton. Clear enough for you, Dan?'

'Perfectly, ma'am.'

'That'll be Reb, Dan. Kind of cute play on my name dreamed up by Jack, me being from Virginia.'

Reb's blue eyes clouded over dreamily.

'When I first met Jack Johnson, a darn Yankee from the roots of his hair to his toenails, I had very different views. But through Jack's example, tolerance and forebearance, he showed me the error of my ways.' She laughed with fond remembrance. 'Back then, Jack even had me believe that there was good in Mame Rockton!'

Reb Johnson's face took on a hard-edged bitterness, which was a darn shame in Dan Tallow's opinion, because it replaced the gentle and pleasant hue of her features with a sour dourness.

'But seeing any good in Rockton, after Abe Rockton passed away and Mame Rockton surrounded herself with men like Spence Barrett, whom Abe wouldn't have let set foot on Rockton range, sorely tested Jack and became impossible for me.'

The lady in question was at that moment looking from behind the acre-sized desk in her den at the gent just mentioned by Reb Johnson, none too pleased with his stewardship. Mame Rockton's grey eyes were chips of ice.

'Reb Johnson got the drop on you?' Her voice reeked of scorn.

Barrett shuffled sheepishly.

'We had that Jew and his rescuer in our sights when the Widder Johnson spiked our guns.' Mame Rockton's scorn turned to outright contempt. 'Nothing we could do, with her holdin' the high ground. She could pick me and the boys off at will, if we tried to nail them.'

Mame Rockton came around the desk, her considerable girth shaking with rage.

'If she had, I'd have gladly paid for your funerals!' She came toe to toe with her foreman. Spence Barrett flinched from the rancher's fury. 'I pay you good money to look after Rockton business,' she fumed, 'and I don't think that you've been earning it!'

Mame Rockton's fury reached a new intensity.

'That Jew can come calling on Beth whenever he's of a mind to. And now we've got this Tallow squatter sitting pretty on Rockton range.'

'He ain't no squatter,' Barrett said in his own defence. 'As I hear it, he's got the deed to the Lowry place.'

Mame Rockton glowered, and Barrett's moment of courage withered.

'If you want, I'll round up the boys and run him

clear out of the valley.'

'Seems to me that Tallow isn't the kind of man to be run off, Spence.'

'We'll plant him then.'

Mame Rockton's mood had changed. She had the sly, snake-eyed look that Spence Barrett had come to know so well in the year he had been her ramrod. He grinned.

'You've got a plan, don't you, boss?'

'Sheriff Metzler sent word that there's a US marshal headed this way. We can't afford to bring attention to ourselves while he's around. My guess is that this marshal's visit is to do with what you and the boys have been getting up to. He might be interested in finding out how the Rockton ranch has grown faster than a summer weed.'

Mame Rockton paced the den, letting her seedling thoughts come to fruition. Then her smile became wily and wolfish.

'I think I've got a plan to get Tallow out of our hair. . . .'

Reb Johnson studied Seth Lowry's deed.

'Well?' Hymie Goldberg asked the Widder Johnson anxiously. 'Is it genuine?'

She went to the window to catch the light, and continued her perusal of the parchment. Her verdict, when she finally delivered it to the two men on tenterhooks, was: 'It's genuine.'

'How do you know?' Dan questioned.

'See this funny mark here?' Tallow and Hymie examined the faded circular mark. 'That's Alice's footprint.'

'Alice?' Tallow asked. 'Who the hell's Alice?'

'Alice was a hog, and for a time Seth Lowry's only friend. Now, when Seth got those copies he'll been doling out to cover his gambling debts printed, Alice's footprint, for some reason, could not be reproduced.'

Reb Johnson held the deed to the light. The faded mark became clearer.

'This is the genuine article all right. You are indeed the new owner of the Lowry place, Dan. Only now, of course, it's officially the Tallow place.'

Hymie Goldberg let out a wild yell of delight.

Dan Tallow's relief was immense. He had feared that just when he had decided to put down roots, they would be torn up again. During the long ride to the valley, he had got more and more used to the idea of abandoning his footloose ways. And since he had set eyes on Reb Johnson, he surely hoped that he could.

As Dan mooned over the very lovely Widder Johnson, Hymie Goldberg's patience ran thinner and thinner.

'We've got a whole heap of work to do, ma'am,' he reminded Reb, none too diplomatically at that, and earned Tallow's scowl of displeasure for his impudence.

Reb Johnson's grin was a wry one.

'I guess you have at that, Hymie,' she said pleasantly. Tallow's relief at her not taking offence at Hymie's less than slick shoehorning of her, was etched in every line of his wind weathered face. 'And I'd best let you gents get to doing it.'

As Reb Johnson headed for the door, Dan Tallow's steely glare settled on Hymie Goldberg, promising a severe rebuke. Hymie was already cringing.

'Ain't no cause for you to hurry off, Reb,' Tallow said. 'Tomorrow will be time enough for Hymie and me to—'

Reb Johnson swung around, her stance one of critical disapproval.

'Hymie is right. Tomorrow is for tomorrow's work, Dan. No point in pushing today's chores into it. It'll surely have enough of its own.'

'Reckoned so, ma'am,' Hymie Goldberg piped up. Now that he had received the Widder Johnson's backing, his glance at Tallow was a cocky one.

Looking round the near-derelict cabin, littered with the debris of Seth Lowry's wayward and lazy life, Reb Johnson offered: 'If you have hunger on you, after you've made a start on making this the Tallow farm, I'd be pleased if you'd drop by the house for washing and grubbing.'

Dan Tallow grinned ear to ear.

'That's a mighty generous gesture, Reb,' he said. 'Hymie and me will sure be along.'

'Not before sunset,' Reb gently scolded Tallow. 'Don't like shirkers. Won't have them in the house.'

'There'll be more moon than sun in the sky, Reb,' Tallow promised.

At the door, Reb said, 'The grub will be simple fare, nothing fancy.'

'I'm sure that anything you'll put on the table will be delicious, Reb.'

'You've got a slick tongue, Dan Tallow,' she chided him. But there was no denying the new spring in her step and glow in her eyes.

Having waved goodbye to Reb, and still grinning from ear to ear, Dan was met by Hymie Goldberg's scoffing stare.

'I swear, Dan, you're acting like a lovesick puppy.'

Dan sighed. 'Ain't the Widder some woman, Hymie?'

'I guess,' Hymie agreed in a throwaway manner. 'But women is the last thing you've got time for right now, Dan Tallow. You've got a farm to find under all this rubbish lying 'round here. So let's get to it.'

Three hours later, as the sun began to sink and the day's toil was over, Dan Tallow massaged his aching back, having been driven harder by Hymie than a stubborn steer on a trail drive, and opined sourly: 'You know what, Hymie, I'm beginning to wonder who the boss is around here?'

Hymie snorted. 'Hah! If you don't know by now, Dan, you must have a hole in your head letting your good sense out.'

Resigned to Hymie Goldberg's brash ways, Tallow mounted his horse to make tracks for Reb Johnson's. At last, having resisted the urge to do so for the previous half-hour, he let his gaze go where he felt the watching eyes from. Spence Barrett and two cronies were on a tree-covered ridge to the south of the farm, sitting and watching, and no doubt planning, too. But planning what? Trouble, Tallow reckoned.

As much trouble as they could brew up.

CHAPTER TEN

In town, Sheriff Lou Metzler was grudgingly answering the US marshal's questions about happenings around Willow Creek and its hinterland, such as the recent death of an old Swede who had fallen foul of Mame Rockton because he had opposed the unlawful expansion of Rockton range. The marshal had arrived two days before he was expected. Metzler, caught on the hop, was not prepared for Marshal Sam Benteen's intense questioning.

'No mystery there,' Metzler bluffed the marshal. 'Hanged himself. Slung a rope over a roof-beam and . . .' Metzler poked out his tongue and made a graphic gesture of having a rope round his neck. 'The Swede was always a tad strange, Marshal.'

'And the burning of the Cleary house here in town?' Benteen pressed.

'Accident. Reckon an overturned oil-lamp, maybe. Happens.'

'Cleary owned the general store, right?' Metzler nodded. 'Mame Rockton offered to buy him out, as she did the Swede?' Metzler nodded again, feeling a tightening of his shirt-collar. 'Only, for a price that was less than a quarter of the store's value in Cleary's case, and the price offered the Swede for his farm was the same.'

'I didn't hear nothin' like that,' Metzler growled.

'I think you did, Sheriff Metzler,' Sam Benteen said gravely. 'In fact, I figure that, for a lawman, you're much too cosy with Mame Rockton.'

Metzler sprang out of his chair, his flabby face suffused with anger; the kind of righteous and blustering spleen that a guilty man often manifests when confronted with his misdeeds.

'That's a real thorny accusation, Marshal!'

'But true, I believe,' Benteen insisted. He held up his hand to stay Metzler's protestation. 'It's late. Tomorrow I intend paying a visit to the Rockton ranch. And if my suspicions are confirmed, which I expect they will be, I'll have your badge, Metzler.'

He paused at the office door before leaving.

'You won't need it breaking rocks,' he added.

Lou Metzler was seething, but he was even more frightened. In a cell behind him, a figure under a blanket stirred.

'Tough *hombre*, isn't he, Lou?'

Metzler spun around. In his anger and worry, he had forgotten the ruse which Mame Rockton had thought up to be privy to Benteen's questioning of him. The US marshal, a careful man, had checked on this prisoner before quizzing Metzler. But on seeing a greasy Stetson at the top of the blanket, and a pair of men's boots poking out the other end, he had been satisfied that Metzler's prisoner was what he said he was, a drunk sleeping off a bender. Mame Rockton's timely grunts and snores had completed the illusion.

'We're done for, for sure,' Metzler panicked.

'Don't give yourself a hernia, Lou,' Mame Rockton soothed. 'Every word the man said is true.'

'So, what're we going to do, Mame?' he asked, wiping the perspiration of fear from his flabby face. 'I don't fancy the idea of breakin' rocks for twenty years. I've gotta come clean, Mame. You can see that, can't you?'

'Could be worse, Lou.' There was no pity in Mame Rockton's grey eyes. 'Benteen could find out that yours was the match that set fire to the Cleary house.'

'Spence Barrett splashed the kerosene,' Metzler whined.

'Doesn't matter. In the eyes of the law, the match-lighter is as guilty as the kerosene-spiller.' Mame Rockton leaned close to Lou Metzler. 'You'd hang for certain.' She strolled casually about the law office, as if she hadn't a care in the world. 'But it isn't going to come to that, Lou.'

'Yeah?' Metzler fretted.

'I've got a plan that will solve all of our problems. That new feller hereabouts. . . .'

'Tallow?'

'That's him.'

'How does he figure, Mame?' Metzler wondered.

'Why, Lou, you'll hang him for the murder of the US marshal.' Mame Rockton laughed. 'And the murders of Cleary and the Swede, of course. Your story will be that Benteen solved the mystery of the deaths, then Tallow, knowing the game was up, bushwhacked him.'

Lou Metzler snorted. 'That won't work, Mame. Tallow wasn't even in these parts then.'

Mame Rockton became impatient with Metzler.

'Who's to know that, back in the territorial capital? You'll be presenting them with the marshal's killer, and a solved mystery. I reckon that they'll close the book, Lou.'

'What if Tallow met folk 'long the way comin' here? They'll be able to testify that he was no way near Willow Creek when the Swede and Cleary were murdered.'

Mame Rockton was untroubled by the sheriff's concerns.

'A drifter, Lou? Who'll remember a passing saddle-tramp? And even if they did, who'd bother saving his neck?'

Metzler was easier in himself, but not completely so.

'And if that doesn't work, then I'll grease a few palms and call in a few favours,' the rancher concluded.

'You could do that right now,' Metzler said hopefully.

'Sure, I could. But that wouldn't get rid of Tallow and that dirty Jew, Hymie Goldberg. With Tallow out of the way, I'll make sure that Goldberg never again bothers Beth.'

'The way I hear it—' Lou Metzler bit off his words, and sweated copiously under Mame Rockton's furious gaze.

'Tell me what you heard, Lou,' she demanded, in a quiet, controlled way.

'Just vicious gossip, Mame.'

'Tell me, damn you!'

Lou Metzler looked about him as if the words that had escaped his mouth could be clutched back.

'I'm waiting, Lou.'

'Well . . . Mame . . . You see, folk are sayin' that Beth . . . Well, Beth kinda encouraged Hymie Goldberg's attentions.'

'Go on,' the rancher urged, icily.

Metzler grimaced as if the devil had him by the tail and was dragging him into Hades. 'That Beth was . . .' He coughed drily. 'Sweet on the Jewboy.'

Mame Rockton's face reflected hellfire. She grabbed a sheet of paper from Metzler's desk and shoved it in his face.

'Names, Lou. Write down every name. When this shindig with the US marshal is over with, I'll have Spence and a couple of the boys call on them to . . . ah . . . straighten out their thinking.'

Fearful that he would be at the top of the Rockton revenge list if he stalled, Metzler began scribbling down names. Finished, he slid the sheet of paper across the desk to the rancher. Picking it up, Mame Rockton ran her eye down the list. Returning her gaze to the cowardly sheriff, she said:

'Don't see Ben's name here, Lou.'

'Ben?' Metzler asked, his voice squeaky.

'Your brother, remember.'

'Sure, Mame. But—'

'But nothing!' the rancher rasped. 'Spence Barrett told me that Ben was mouthing off in the saloon only last week about Beth and Hymie Goldberg. I've been meaning to pay a call on him since then.' She shoved the sheet of paper back across the desk.

'Ben can't hold his liquor, Mame.'

'Nor his tongue, either.'

'He meant no harm. I'll talk to him, Mame. Whop him if you want.'

'Put his name on the list, Lou,' the rancher insisted. Her smile was pure evil. 'After all, we wouldn't want folk saying that Rockton justice was twisted, now, would we?'

'Guess not, Mame,' he muttered.

Head bowed, Lou Metzler added his brother's name to the list.

Mame Rockton folded the sheet of paper and shoved it into her left boot.

'Now, about snaring this Tallow *hombre*, Lou. . . .'

CHAPTER ELEVEN

At that moment, the nostrils of the man being discussed in Metzler's office were getting the drift of freshly baked apple pie on the southerly breeze blowing over Reb Johnson's house. Hymie Goldberg, a couple of paces adrift of Dan Tallow, licked lips that food had not passed for the best part of two days. Intertwined with the smell of apple pie, was the mouthwatering aroma of roast beef. And when Reb Johnson came to the door to greet them, smelling sweetly, her perfume was the perfect balance in an overall heady mix.

Reb was out of jeans and into a red silk dress that Satan had designed to tempt, showing as it did her shapely form. Tallow's breath left him in a single gasp and his senses reeled with the pleasure the sight of Reb Johnson gave him. Women he had known a-plenty, but he was certain that of all the women he had known, Reb Johnson was a woman apart; a woman he would gladly and willingly forfeit his soul to possess.

'Howdy, Reb,' Dan greeted, and hoped that the quiver in his voice did not reveal the fire in his groin. 'You surely look a picture.'

'Like I said, Dan, you're a slick-tongued one to be sure.'

But beneath her blustery and feisty retort, Reb Johnson's heart fluttered in a way that it had not fluttered in a long time. She both hated and loved the giddy feeling running across her belly. Hated it because of the sense of guilt and betrayal it brought, and loved it for the reawakening of her womanhood that it had triggered. It had been a hell of a long time since a man had had the effect that Dan Tallow was having on her. And she had honestly never expected any man after Jack Johnson to raise in her the kind of fire that was now relentlessly rolling through her.

'Dan's right,' Hymie Goldberg said. 'You're a real looker, Mrs Johnson.'

Up to that second, Reb Johnson had managed to control her blushes. She quickly turned back inside the house.

'What did you say that for?' Tallow challenged his young partner.

'Why not? It's true. You said so yourself.'

'Me saying so is different!'

'How do you figure that?' Hymie questioned. 'I'm a man, too.'

'Just take my word for it, Hymie. It's different.

So, from now on, any complimenting that's to be done, I'll do it.'

'Ornery critter, ain't you?' Bewildered, Hymie Goldberg shook his head. 'I'll be blowed if I'll ever get to understand you, Dan Tallow.'

'Grub's getting cold,' Reb called from inside the house.

Before going in, Dan again reminded Hymie about his role as the master complimenter.

Watching, Spence Barrett and his cronies were eaten up with jealousy and nagged by darker emotions.

'Just a day in the damn valley,' a man called Luke Croft growled meanly, 'and that feller Tallow's on his way to Reb Johnson's bed.'

Spence Barrett snorted. 'Well, a doomed man is entitled to a last romp, fellas.'

Their laughter was humourless. The imaginings of what Dan Tallow had in store for him allowed for no goodwill towards him.

'Best get back to the ranch,' Barrett, the Rockton foreman, said. 'I've got some jawing to do with the boss about Tallow's future.'

Luke Croft sniggered. 'Future, Spence? What future? Tallow ain't got one.'

Spence Barrett pointed his horse towards the Rockton range, enjoying Croft's observations.

'Ain't that a fact, Luke?' he said.

The meal over, Dan Tallow sat back in his chair a pleased man. Hymie Goldberg, with the appetite of a youngster, took another ten minutes to pack himself with as much grub as his stomach could take in before bursting wide open.

'That, Reb,' Tallow complimented, 'was the best grub I've ever tasted.'

Hymie Goldberg's contented sigh spoke more than a thousand complimentary words.

Reb Johnson, her eyes a touch misty, said softly: 'It's good to have a man to cook for again, Dan.'

For once, Hymie Goldberg's mouth waited for his brain to think.

'You know,' he said, standing up, stretching and yawning, 'I'm pretty beat. I reckon I'll head back to the farm, Dan.'

'You're welcome to stay, Hymie,' Reb invited. 'Until that cabin is half decent for a body to live in.'

His eyes met Tallow's, and the message in Dan's was crystal clear.

'I'd hate to impose, ma'am. The cabin will be just fine.'

Reb Johnson's eyes clashed with Tallow's, uncertainty stalking them.

'The house isn't big enough for you . . . b-both,' she stammered. 'But the barn's cosy,' she told Hymie. Hymie glanced Dan's way for his approval before accepting Reb Johnson's generous offer. Cramping a man's play, when his hopes were writ-

81

ten across his forehead for all to see, was not his style. Most times the antics between men and women confused him. Though with the feelings he had for Beth Rockton and the risks he took to snatch a few moments with her, he was beginning to understand the age-old rituals of the mating game.

Getting Dan's approval, he chirped: 'Obliged, ma'am.'

'You'll find blankets in that press near the fire.'

'Blankets, too,' Hymie yelped delightedly. 'Dang, you're really spoiling me something awful, Mrs Johnson.'

Reb Johnson was obviously pleased with Hymie Goldberg's genuine enthusiasm and fulsome gratitude.

'And if you go through the kitchen on your way out, you'll find apple pie to keep the hunger pangs away during the night.'

Hymie's eyes lit up. 'Apple pie, too,' he said in wonder. 'More than a Jew deserves around these parts, ma'am.'

'Jew. Christian. Non-believer. Makes no difference to me, Hymie.'

'That's what makes you really special, ma'am,' Hymie said with sincerity. 'See you come sun-up, Dan.'

Reb Johnson's eyes hit the floor. Tallow glared at a cringing Hymie.

'Sun-up?' he joked. 'You leave room in the barn for me, Hymie.'

'Sure, Dan.' Hymie scurried off to the kitchen.

The silence between Reb Johnson and Dan Tallow lasted a long time, neither able to find the words to bridge the gap prised open by Hymie Goldberg's unthinking remarks. It was Reb who finally spoke.

Her words, though welcome and kind, did nothing to clarify the undercurrents flowing between them.

'Hymie's a nice boy, isn't he, Dan?'

'A bit mouthy sometimes,' Tallow observed.

'That's what being young is all about, isn't it?'

'I guess,' he agreed.

'Think back and you'll recall a thousand times when a shut mouth would have been a whole lot better and wiser than an open one,' she laughed.

The silence crept back, and stood between them like a grudging ghost. This time it fell to Dan to break the impasse, and knowing that he was not a man who could use fancy words to cloak the kernel of what he was about to say, he spoke bluntly.

'Reb, I guess there's no doubt in *your* mind about what's in *my* mind.' Reb Johnson flushed. 'So I'd appreciate it if you'd tell me, should I howl at the moon, or crawl out of here with my tail firmly between my legs?'

Flustered, Reb rebuked, 'You don't mince your words, Dan Tallow!'

'Don't know many words to mince, so I always figured that I'd make myself plain with the words I do know, Reb.'

Reb Johnson laughed. 'How about a compromise?' she suggested.

'Compromise? What have you got in mind, Reb?' he asked, stepping on eggs.

'This . . .' She leaned over and kissed Dan on the right cheek. 'To take to the barn with you.'

Dan Tallow's fingers went to his face where Reb had kissed him. He said: 'I don't aim to give up, Reb.'

'And I don't think I'll want you to, Dan. But I want to be sure that when we finally get together, *if* we get together,' she cautioned, 'that it will be from work done rather than hormonal expediency.'

Dan Tallow's eyebrows shot up.

'Hor*what*? Ex*what*?'

Reb Johnson took him by the arm and guided him to the door. 'You'll have lots of time before sun-up to figure it out, Dan,' she said, a mischievous smile on her lips. 'You won't be getting much sleep.' Closing the door on him, she sighed. 'And neither will I.'

Shortly before first light, after a long, restless and tossing night, Dan Tallow smiled and murmured: 'Hor*what*? Ex*what*, huh? Yeah,' he sighed, 'I guess I know what you mean all right, Reb.'

Woken by a shaft of light across his eyes through a crack in the barn wall, Hymie Goldberg looked at

Tallow through sleepy eyes, surprised to find that Dan had shared the barn with him.

'Things didn't work out with Reb Johnson, huh?' he asked.

Dan thought about Hymie's question for a moment, before concluding, 'Oh, they worked out just dandy, Hymie.'

Puzzled, Hymie said, 'Then how come you're here in the barn?'

'In the flesh, Hymie,' Dan sighed. 'But in spirit I was with Reb every second of the night.' Hymie's puzzlement deepened. Tallow asked, 'Who did you dream of, Hymie?'

'Beth Rockton, of course,' Hymie answered, without the slightest hesitation. Slowly, Hymie Goldberg's confusion cleared. 'Yeah, Dan.' His smile was easy and slow. 'Know what you mean.'

'Ain't love a darn strange thing, Hymie?' Dan Tallow pondered.

Contentedly, Hymie agreed. 'Strange, yeah, but wonderful, Dan.'

His dreaminess overcome by hunger, Hymie Goldberg began to scatter the bed of straw he had slept on.

'Now, where the hell did I put that slice of apple pie?'

CHAPTER TWELVE

'How're you planning on getting Tallow to come to town?' Spence Barrett asked Mame Rockton.

'By spreading the word about a big blackjack game,' the rancher said, obviously pleased with the slickness of her planning. 'Tallow won the Lowry farm in a blackjack game, which tells me that he's a card-playing gent. Right now he must be needing a stake pretty bad. He'll need supplies for the winter. I'm betting that blackjack, as a way to get that stake, will prove irresistible to Tallow.'

The Rockton foreman hated to throw cold water on his boss's plan, but if the plan went wrong, he could end up breaking rocks or swinging on a gallows. So he abandoned his normal caution to remind Mame of something.

'Tallow won't come to town. Not after the last skirmish. He'll reckon that he'd be walking into the lion's den, and he's no fool.'

Mame Rockton glared at her foreman, angry that he should have the slightest doubt about her proficiency in planning mayhem.

'That's why you'll be riding over to the Tallow farm to make your peace with him, Spence.'

'What?' Barrett yelled. 'I ain't going no way near Tallow, unless it's to string up that Jew boy and him!'

'Whose dollars are in your pocket?' the rancher barked. 'Rockton dollars, that's whose dollars they are. And if you don't want to earn them, you can always hit the trail.'

Spence Barrett knew that he had overstepped the mark with Mame Rockton, and he quickly pulled in his horns.

'Yes, ma'am,' he said. 'You're the boss round here.'

'Well, what are you waiting for then?'

Barrett gladly hurried from the room, oblivious to everything. His concentration was solely on getting through the front door and out of the house, so that he could breathe again to rid his legs of the jelly in them.

The foreman's dogged departure was a stroke of good fortune for Beth Rockton, who, caught unawares by the suddenness of Spence Barrett's exit from her stepmother's presence, had had no time to flee along the hall or upstairs. All she had time to do was step behind the outward-opening room door, and when Barrett flicked it shut, hope that he would not look behind him.

Beth sagged against the wall with relief when the foreman slammed the front door behind him without looking back. Then, and only then, did the import of what she had heard fully register with Beth Rockton. She had had many disagreements with her stepmother about the way that Rockton business was conducted, knowing that it would not have been her late father's wish that Rockton expansion should be at the expense of the neighbours, and she felt that honest dealing should be the Rockton hallmark. Not a day went by without Beth missing her father, Abe, and she was missing him more and more.

Forced to spend most of her time in the house on the pretence that a young lady should not mix with the kind of riff-raff that a ranch crew was made up of, Beth had not, up until a couple of minutes ago, realized how evil her stepmother's actions were. She had heard Spence Barrett and Mame coolly discussing murder, like one might the everyday business of running the ranch. A man by the name of Dan Tallow was to be framed for the murder of a man called Benteen. But what could she do about it? If she revealed what she had heard, it would mean the incarceration of her stepmother, or worse. And if she kept secret about what she had overheard, it would mean that one innocent man was murdered and another, Tallow, would hang for that murder.

'Oh, Hymie, my love,' she fretted. 'If only you were here, you could tell me what to do. Where are you, Hymie, when I need you most?'

Breakfast over with, Dan Tallow and Hymie Goldberg took their leave of Reb Johnson, but Reb's insistence that they should both return for supper and board made the parting that much easier for Tallow. It would be a long day, in which he would count the seconds to set eyes on Reb again, but he was now determined that the farm would return to what a farm should be, and that soon he would come and collect Reb and take her to look at its redemption and share in his pride. Riding away, Tallow decided that that would be the day when he would ask Reb Johnson to become Reb Tallow.

When they reached the farm, a journey through which Hymie Goldberg, unable to breach Tallow's dreamy reverie, talked to himself, he leapt back out of the cabin on seeing Spence Barrett sitting at the rickety table. Instantly, eyes wide with alarm, Hymie looked around him for sight of other Rockton hardcases. There were none, and when Barrett came to the cabin door to greet Tallow, his mood was one of bonhomie and good neigh-bourliness.

On seeing Barrett, Tallow's mood soured.

'What are you doing here, Barrett?' he ques-

tioned the Rockton ramrod sternly, his hand dropping to his sixgun.

'Paying a visit and mending bridges, Tallow,'
Barrett said, in as friendly a manner as Hymie
Goldberg would never have thought possible.

'Yeah?'

Tallow remained on alert.

'With Hymie, too,' Barrett said.

'Huh?' Hymie Goldberg yelped. 'You want to be
friends with me?'

Spence Barrett threw out his hands. 'It's time to
settle this valley and live as neighbours should. In
friendship and harmony.'

'You're full of moonshine, ain't you?' Hymie
charged.

Barrett laughed the way an old friend accus-
tomed to another friend's joshing might.

'Ain't tasted moonshine in a year. Not since the
Swede hanged himself. He could make real good
moonshine.'

'The Swede did *not* hang himself, Barrett,'
Hymie Goldberg stubbornly insisted.

Spence Barrett shrugged. 'That was Sheriff
Metzler's verdict, Hymie.'

'Metzler's as twisted as a crawling rattlesnake!
And even more a Mame Rockton lackey than you
are, Barrett.'

Promising himself that when the time came,
Hymie Goldberg would die a breath at a time, and
seeing no way that he could fool Goldberg, the

Rockton foreman returned to persuading Dan Tallow of his good intentions, laughing inside all the time.

'Don't you agree that it's time to set our grievances aside, Tallow?'

Dan Tallow looked to Hymie Goldberg.

'Don't you believe one word from this devil's lips, Dan,' Hymie warned.

'Look, I know that it'll take time for you to come round to seeing me as your friend, Hymie,' Barrett cajoled, 'and I don't blame you.' His attention returned to Dan. 'I'm trying real hard to make amends, Tallow. But I'll need your help and co-operation to forge a new beginning.'

'Don't listen, Dan,' Hymie urged.

Tallow, lacking Hymie Goldberg's knowledge of how evil a man Spence Barrett was, saw Hymie's tempestuous rebuff as one of youthful rage rather than an older man's wisdom. He said: 'I'll give it a try, Barrett.'

Hymie pleaded, 'You can't make friends with a snake, Dan.'

But Tallow, growing impatient with what he saw as Hymie Goldberg's intransigence, repeated: 'I'm willing to give it a try, Barrett.'

As he shook Tallow's hand, Barrett's grin was wide. 'You'll see that it's for the best.' Before hitting the trail, he told Dan: 'I've told the boys that if you and Hymie come to town for supplies or pleasure, you're not to be bothered in any way.'

'I appreciate your advocacy,' Tallow said.

When he rode away, Spence Barrett began the second phase of Mame Rockton's plan for Dan Tallow's demise. He made his way up a mountain track to a Rockton line shack, where the man Mame Rockton had hired and rigged out to act as the gambler, who would drop by the Tallow farm to inform Tallow casually of the big blackjack game planned in town that night, was waiting.

'You be sure to convince him,' Barrett warned the man. 'And don't put in an appearance for a couple of hours yet. We wouldn't want Tallow thinking that the day had too much good fortune in it. That's the kind of day that makes a man suspicious that fate might be of an impish frame of mind.'

Spence Barrett rode back to the Rockton ranch well pleased, to assure Mame Rockton that the groundwork for Dan Tallow's downfall had been completed. And by that fact, so also was Hymie Goldberg's end near at hand.

The day's work, once Tallow soothed Hymie Goldberg's ruffled feathers, went well, and it was late evening when Dan took a breather and saw the fancily dressed rider approaching, hat off and rubbing the sweat from his brow. Dan thought this a touch unusual. The man had gambler written all over him, and in Dan Tallow's experience that species of workshy gent was adverse to perspiring.

'Howdy,' the rider greeted Tallow. 'I'm some-what parched. Mind if I step over to your well for a drink?'

'Not at all,' Dan replied, letting his eyes wander over the visitor's dusty but well-cut clothes. 'Come far?'

Hand-cupping water from the well bucket, the stranger informed Tallow: 'From Larksville.'

'Larksville? I'm as new as a babe in these parts myself. Could you put miles on that for me?'

'It's a town about twenty miles south of here. A cow town.'

Where else would a gambler be found, Tallow thought. Cow towns had lots of gullible trail crews who could be parted from their hard-earned wages without too much difficulty.

'Ain't much round here to interest a gent of your, ah . . . *profession*,' Tallow said.

The gambler chuckled. 'You musn't be a card-playing man, sir, if you haven't heard about the big blackjack game in town tonight.'

Dan Tallow's ears pricked. 'Blackjack game, you say?'

'Sure. I hope to ride away from town with a healthy poke. Play blackjack?' he casually enquired of Dan.

'A time or two.'

'Well, I'd best be making tracks to town. Get a little shuteye before tonight's big game.'

Dan Tallow thought, a man needs to be alert

with a couple of spare aces up his sleeve. But he quickly scattered his unkind thoughts. He had never set eyes on the gambler before and knew nothing of his style of playing. He might, though he doubted it very much, be talking to the one honest gambler in the West.

'Thanks for the water. Maybe you'll drop by town and we'll meet again?'

'Maybe,' Tallow said, not showing much interest, but he was full of a fiery excitement inside.

The gambler was barely out of earshot when Hymie Goldberg quizzed Tallow: 'You ain't thinking of joining that game, are you?'

'We need a stake, Hymie,' Tallow reasoned. 'And blackjack's my game.'

'Blackjack ain't no one's game, Dan,' Hymie protested. 'Not like poker, where knowhow and skill is needed.'

'Learn to read the faces around a blackjack table, and the pot is yours, Hymie,' Tallow said.

'Then how come a fella like Seth Lowry lost everything he owned on the turn of a blackjack card?'

'He never learned to read the faces round the table, Hymie.'

Hymie asked sceptically, 'Played a lot of blackjack, Dan?'

'A whole pile.'

'Then how come all you've got to show for it is a weak-legged nag and the shirt on your back?'

Grim-faced, Dan Tallow replied, 'You know, Hymie, you can be a definite depresser of a man's spirits!'

'You're going to town, ain't you?'

'Well. . . .'

'What about the Widder Johnson? She'll have grub waiting.'

'Reb will understand,' Tallow piped up, wishing he was as sure as he pretended to be. 'She's a practical woman who'll know the value of getting a stake.'

'A practical woman, sure enough, who sees hard work as the way to prosperity and card-playing as the road to damnation.'

Doubt took hold of Tallow.

'You figure, Hymie?'

'I figure, Dan. I reckon that you could throw away in one swoop all the good work you've put in with Reb Johnson. Are you willing to risk that for a game of blackjack? And what if you run into Spence Barrett and his cronies?'

'That's not a problem any more, Hymie. You heard Barrett. He cleared it with his crew for me to go to town any time I like.'

'You believe what Barrett says?' Hymie asked, bewildered by Tallow's *naïveté*. 'You ride into town, and you might as well save Barrett the trouble and shoot yourself right here and now.'

'Barrett doesn't trouble me none,' Tallow said airily. Then, worriedly: 'But earning Reb

Johnson's disapproval would.'

'Then stay away from town,' Hymie Goldberg advised.

After careful consideration of Hymie's advice, Tallow conceded: 'I guess you're right, Hymie.'

'I know I am,' Hymie said emphatically. 'So, let's put in another hour or so, and then we'll clean up and head over to Reb Johnson's for supper.'

However, an hour that had begun diligently, slowly turned to one of shifty unease for Dan Tallow. He had visions of a great big pot that would buy the supplies he so badly needed. Eating and sleeping at Reb Johnson's place was mighty pleasurable, but his newfound pride and independence would prefer him to be visiting Reb's on the footing of a man who was not dependent on charity, which he would be for a long time to come without that all important stake.

Hymie Goldberg, observing Tallow's growing restlessness, said: 'You're going, ain't you?'

Knowing that pretence was no longer a viable option, Tallow said: 'I'm going, Hymie. I can't pass up on a chance to get a poke together.'

'Or lose what little you've got,' Hymie reminded him.

'What I've got doesn't make a difference anyway,' Dan flung back, defensive under Hymie's disappointed study of him. 'Tell Reb—'

'Tell her *what*, Dan?' Hymie challenged. 'A great whopping lie?' He shook his head. 'Reb saved our hides, fed and provided a bed for us. She's been too kind to us to lie to her. And I don't aim to do that. Even for you, Dan.'

Desperate, Tallow said: 'I saved your hide too, Hymie, or have you forgotten that?'

The setting sun shadowing Hymie Goldberg's dark features could not hide his deep hurt.

'That I'll always be beholden to you for, Dan. But I still won't lie to Reb Johnson for you.'

After a moment's angry consideration of Hymie's principled stand, Tallow's mood softened. 'You know, Hymie,' he said solemnly, 'I reckon that you're the most principled cuss I've ever crossed paths with. And I figure, too, that Mame Rockton could do a whole lot worse than have you as a son-in-law.'

'Son-in-law!' Hymie exploded. 'Danged if I'd want Mame Rockton for a mother-in-law. Be like having Satan himself as kin!'

'Marry Beth Rockton and that's what Mame will be,' Dan said.

Hymie Goldberg's gaze became dreamy, and his eyes looked a long way into the distance and the future. He vowed: 'If Beth and me tie the knot, Dan, we'll go far away from this place or anyone called Rockton.'

Dan Tallow sounded a note of caution: 'Beth might not see it that way, Hymie.'

'Given the chance, I'll persuade her that it's for the best.'

'Where would you go?'

Hymie's brown eyes misted over. 'Some place where a man can be a Jew without someone wanting to hang him or shoot him for it.'

Dan Tallow did not dampen Hymie Goldberg's dreams by telling him that finding such a place would not be easy. At least not before he had to climb and suffer the indignity of a whole mountain of ignorant bigotry.

Heading for his horse, Dan said, 'Explain to Reb, will you, Hymie?'

'I'll try, Dan. Don't know if I can.'

Hymie watched Tallow ride off into the sunset until he vanished from sight. He looked around him at the work of the day; sizeable progress it was, too. But his joy was smothered by a dreary and dark foreboding. And the hope that his partnership with Dan Tallow had brought him, had lost most of its sparkle.

He mounted up and headed for the Johnson farm, spending his time trying to find the words that would save some of Dan Tallow's undoubted good standing with Reb Johnson, while at the same time saving Reb's feelings, too. Because, though he'd be the first to admit that he had a long way to go before he fully understood the mating game, he did know enough to realize that as taken as Dan Tallow had been with Reb Johnson, she was even more sparked by him.

When Reb came to the door, breathless and

looking as beautiful as only a woman in love can look, Hymie Goldberg's heart dropped into his boots.

'Howdy, Hymie,' she greeted him, but absently so, her eyes searching the dark behind him, eager to glimpse Tallow. When she could not catch sight of him, her questioning eyes settled on Hymie, who silently cursed Dan for the hurt his absence was about to inflict on Reb Johnson.

Beth Rockton's blue eyes darted about every which way at the plethora of moving shadows, and her ears exaggerated every sound until she sat brittle in the saddle. Maybe, she thought, it would have been wiser to have taken the direct trail to the old Lowry place, where she had heard the ranch hands say that Hymie had thrown in his lot with this fellow Tallow, who was giving her stepma and Spence Barrett so much worry.

To avoid prying eyes, she had chosen a trail through a long stretch of pine for the cover it would give her, almost to Tallow's door. But now that the grey light in which she had set out had finally faded into the pitch blackness of a moonless night, Beth was beginning to be haunted by the ghosts in her mind. And there was also the danger of being thrown. The ground was full of tree stumps and brush in which her horse's legs could easily become entangled. Great holes where the roots of trees had been ripped from the soil either by nature or man, were also an ever-present danger to a safe passage. When she finally crested a rise and saw the outline of the Lowry place, or rather the Tallow farm now, her relief was palpable. But she was wise enough to avoid a hasty descent from the hill, despite the urgency of her warning for Dan Tallow about her stepmother's plans to bring about his doom.

But an even greater urgency had to be resisted, and that was the burning desire to see and be with Hymie Goldberg.

When she reached the deserted cabin, Beth Rockton's heart sank. Now she was faced with the stark choice of returning to the ranch and letting a man be killed and another be unjustly accused of his murder, or continuing on to town to tell Sheriff Metzler about the awful deeds planned for that night. If she did that, it would mean a whole heap of trouble for her stepmother. But, in essence, if she were not to be party to murder, what else could she do but tell the sheriff? And was it not better anyway for her stepmother to be hauled over the coals for *planning* a murder, rather than having the killing done?

Beth had little respect for her stepmother, and no love at all. She had, while her pa was alive, pretended to care for Mame Rockton. But when her pa had died, Beth saw no further reason to pretend. Neither, for that matter, had her stepmother. The fact was, the sooner she could get free of Mame Rockton's clutches and be with Hymie Goldberg, the better she'd like it.

Her young shoulders heavy with concern, Beth Rockton headed for town.

CHAPTER THIRTEEN

On seeing Dan Tallow put in an appearance, Sheriff Lou Metzler slipped out the back door of the law office and made fast tracks through the town's backlots to the rear of the Tipperary Shamrock saloon, where he let himself in. Once inside the narrow hallway, he quickly sought out the small, cluttered room that served as an office, where Spence Barrett and a party of trusted town cronies (using his regular bunch of Rockton hard-cases might alert Tallow to danger) were holed up, along with the man playing the role of the professional gambler.

Bursting into the room, Metzler announced: 'Tallow's here!'

Instantly, on Metzler delivering his news, the anxiously waiting men hurried away to the main saloon to take their positions at the card table. Other men bellied up to the bar and sat at tables, all players in the charade to nail Tallow. Most of the men lit up fat cigars and puffed volumes of smoke in the air, to give the impression that the men were long-haul imbibers and card-players.

Spence Barrett took from his vest pocket the roll of dollar bills which Mame Rockton had provided him with as part of the scheme to lure Tallow. He distributed eye-catching bundles of bills to the players, so that when Tallow entered the saloon he could not fail but to be impressed. Barrett also provided the hefty pot, which, just as Tallow entered the Tipperary Shamrock, one of Barrett's trusted cronies would be hauling in, to give the impression that the professional gambler in their midst was not having it all his own way. A lot of men would not sit in on a game with a professional card-player, feeling that the odds would be stacked against them by the gambler's skill at reading the game, or more than likely by his guile at manipulating the deck.

A man at the window alerted Barrett to Dan Tallow's imminent arrival, and, with perfect timing, the man chosen to win the pot was hauling it in just as Tallow stepped inside. With a sly glance, Spence Barrett saw the flash of interest in Dan's eyes, and knew that all of his preparation and staging was about to pay off. Under the table he slipped the man playing the role of the gambler a new deck of rigged cards, the sequence of which when dealt, would give Tallow the winning hand.

Barrett looked around, and seeing Tallow imme-diately invited him to join the game.

On the journey to town, Tallow's participation could have gone either way, torn as he was between his desire for a winning hand that would give him the stake he so badly needed, and his desire not to displease Reb Johnson. However, seeing the pot which the man had just hauled in and the healthy stacks of bills round the table for the taking, his resistance melted.

'Don't know if I could stay in the game for very long, Spence,' Dan said. 'A couple of bad hands would see me busted.'

'You might be lucky,' the Rockton foreman said. 'Won't know 'til you try.'

Spence Barrett pushed out the chair nearest to him, the only vacant chair at the table, positioned to match the deal of the rigged deck to give Tallow the winning cards. When Dan sat down, the second phase of the scheme to have him hanged as the killer of US Marshal Sam Benteen kicked in.

The gambler dealt.

Quickly, all of the players with the exception of Barrett, the gambler and Dan, threw in their hands. Barrett pretended to sweat for a spell, then swore and threw down his hand.

'Mister?' The gambler's gaze settled on Tallow.

Dan, feeling sweat trickle down his back, looked at the Nine of Spades and the Ten of Diamonds he held. His gaze wandered to the sizeable bet. It was a good hand, but was it good enough? What would be his chances of getting a two? Slim, he reckoned. He resisted the urge to try and enhance his chances of winning.

'I'll play these,' he said.

The gambler turned his first card – Queen of Clubs.

Dan's heart thumped.

The gambler fingered his second card, toying with Dan.

'Turn the damn card, gambler!' a man at the table growled, acting out his part to perfection.

'What do you reckon it might be?' the gambler asked Dan, his smile slick.

The protest around the table grew. The gambler held up his hands.

'OK. OK!'

He turned his second card. Dan's heart settled down some when he saw the Five of Hearts.

'Anyone like a side bet?' the gambler asked.

'What kinda side bet?' The question came from Spence Barrett.

'Say a hundred, that I'll turn a six on this fifteen.'

'That's a loco bet,' the man who had earlier protested at the gambler's delay in turning his second card snorted.

Everything was working as smoothly as the spring of a cuckoo clock. Spence Barrett was a well-pleased man.

The buckshee gambler shrugged. 'I'm a gambler.'

'Are you serious?' the Rockton foreman quizzed the gambler, knowing well that his impromptu bet was all part of the plan.

'I'm serious,' the gambler assured Spence Barrett.

'I'll take your bet,' was the chorus round the table.

'The more in, the more to be gained,' the gambler crooned.

'Dan,' Barrett invited Tallow, 'you in?'

Dan looked at the hundred dollars he had on the table. Should he risk it all on the gambler's side bet? Or maybe be prudent and risk only part of it? On the face of it, the odds against the gambler turning a six were good – very good. That was, of course, if the gambler was dealing from an honest deck. But he had been watching the gambler, and he had seen no hint of chicanery on his part. In fact, he would swear that the gambler's deal was an honest one.

Mouth dry, Dan pushed the hundred dollars into the side bet.

Eyes riveted on the gambler to spot any sleight of hand, Dan Tallow held his breath. He had seen a hundred and one gamblers' tricks at card tables from the Yukon to the Mexican border, but there was always one more.

'Deal,' Spence Barrett eagerly requested of the gambler.

106

The gambler flicked a card. Dan Tallow saw no trickery. The card spun in the air. Eyes strained to get a glimpse of it. The card dropped on the table and stood on its edge for a second before revealing itself. The Tipperary Shamrock erupted in wild jubilation as the spinning card was the Nine of Clubs.

'Win some, lose some,' the gambler observed philosophically.

Dan yahooed and cheered with the men round the table. He had won an extra hundred dollars on the side bet, and an end of the rainbow bet, too.

Spence Barrett reached out and swept Dan's winnings to him.

If Dan had not been avariciously eyeing the sea of dollar bills in front of him, he would have seen, and would probably have understood, the sly exchange of glances between Spence Barrett and the men round the table.

CHAPTER FOURTEEN

The next hand, though not as healthy as the last, also went Dan's way. Spence Barrett was generous in his goodwill towards him. Dan would never have suspected that, based on his initial assessment of Barrett's character, he would have it in him to bury old scores, but it looked so. Tallow's fooling was a compliment to the Rockton ramrod's skill as an actor. Of course, Dan was at the disadvantage of not knowing Spence Barrett as well as Reb Johnson or Hymie Goldberg did. And his big mistake was in not heeding Hymie's warning about Barrett's snake-in-the-grass nature.

'Seems that you're all set to clean us out, Dan,' Barrett said amiably, and called to the bar: 'Whiskey, keeper.'

The barkeep bent under the counter and picked up the specially doctored bottle of whiskey, which he swiftly delivered to the table. Barrett poured a generous measure for Dan, who gulped it down.

'Success makes a man thirsty, eh, Dan?' Mame Rockton's chief henchman joked.

He poured a second, and even more generous, measure of whiskey.

The slimy Mexican watching from the shadows at the back of the saloon smiled knowingly. Rico Suarez's features told of his Apache blood, and it was his knowledge of potions, learned from the Apache medicine men, which would make Dan Tallow pliable for betrayal.

Barrett did not know what roots or plants Suarez used for his concoctions, because the Mexican closely guarded his secrets. But he had seen the effects of Suarez's witchery several times, and had marvelled at its potency.

Rico Suarez had done Mame Rockton many services with his mind-twisting devilry. Tonight's potion would make Tallow angry and argumentative, the exact mood Barrett wanted him in to complete his downfall.

Soon after drinking the whiskey, the saloon and its occupants began to take on all sorts of weird shapes that Dan found increasingly annoying and threatening. He felt an anger well up inside him for no reason that he could discern.

Sheriff Lou Metzler, who had been waiting in the wings for his cue, now stepped in to the

Tipperary Shamrock and ordered the game to break up. He yanked Tallow's chair from under him, pitching him to the floor, from where he came up snarling.

'Are you looking for trouble, Tallow?' Metzler growled. ' 'Cause if you are, bucko . . .' The crooked lawman's hand dropped to hover over his sixgun.

Spence Barrett stepped in. 'Dan's just had one too many, Lou.'

However, with the Mexican's potion now coursing through his veins, all reason had, as Barrett expected, deserted Tallow, and he clumsily went to draw on Metzler. Though awkward of hand, Dan's speed, an unknown quantity, had not been planned for, and Metzler was caught cold until the Rockton ramrod's gun clipped Dan on the skull from behind. Tallow reeled across the saloon to crash heavily against the bar.

Quick to take advantage of the situation, Barrett declared: 'Damn it, Tallow! No need for gunplay.' He stormed across the saloon and grappled with Dan. Hauling him roughly to his feet, Barrett threw him out on to the street. 'You be careful, Sheriff,' he said. 'That darn fool's in a killing mood.'

Mame Rockton's henchman was well pleased with himself. His plan to see Dan Tallow dangling on a rope was progressing even better than he had planned.

Shaken, because he had looked death in the face, Lou Metzler left the saloon on rubber legs. But he was not the only man to depart. Seconds before, under cover of the bust-up, another man had slipped out the back way and had made quick tracks to the hotel, where just then he was knocking gently on Marshal Sam Benteen's door, careful not to draw attention to his presence. The last thing he wanted was for some curious occupant of another room to poke his head out. The room door opened a crack. Benteen was a cautious man. Many of his colleagues had opened doors without due care and had ended up dead.

'What do you want, mister?' the US marshal enquired gruffly of his visitor, slanting his view to check on the hall either side of the caller, to make sure, in as far as he could, that he was alone.

The man spun his well-rehearsed yarn about being on an errand for a prominent citizen who had evidence that would bring to book the people whom the marshal had come to investigate, and about Lou Metzler's connivance in their crimes.

'He's waiting in the alley near the general store to hand over all this evidence, Marshal,' his visitor informed Benteen.

'In the alley near the general store, huh?' Benteen questioned sceptically. 'Why didn't this prominent citizen bring this evidence here to the hotel? Or give it to you to deliver?'

'This is a Rockton town, Marshal. If anyone saw

him visit you, and then Mame Rockton was corralled. . . . Well, the Rockton reach is long and vengeful. Can't blame him for being careful, can you?'

Benteen had to concede the sound sense of his visitor's reasoning. In his time as a lawman, he had seen the power of the big ranchers to intimidate folk.

'Makes sense, I guess,' he said. 'This wouldn't be the first meeting I've had in a dark alley.'

Satisfied that his role in Dan Tallow's snaring had been completed, the man left, reminding Benteen. 'He's kinda nervous hanging round in that alley, Marshal. Won't wait long.'

His visitor barely out of sight, Benteen set his misgivings aside. Exposing and punishing Rockton treachery was always going to be risky. He grabbed his hat and buckled on his gunbelt.

As Dan Tallow picked himself up off Main and wandered aimlessly, the town spinning, he was grabbed and pulled into the alley alongside the general store. By now, Rico Suarez's potion had taken full effect, and he offered no resistance to his handler.

With Tallow barely out of sight, Sam Benteen came from the hotel. He paused to check the deserted street. Satisfied that his passage would both be safe and go unnoticed, he hurried along Main. On reaching the appointed meeting-place, he edged up to the corner of the alley and peered into the pitch blackness.

'I'm Sam Benteen,' he said. 'You wanted to see me?'

'Thought you'd never get here, Marshal,' a man's fretful voice answered from the dark alley. 'I've got all you'll ever need to nail Mame Rockton and her henchmen right here.'

'Bring it to me,' Benteen instructed.

'Can't do that,' the man said. 'There are Rockton eyes everywhere in this burg. If you want it, you come and get it, Marshal.'

Sam Benteen's anxiety to get his hands on the evidence the man claimed he had, overrode his caution. Still, he stepped warily into the alley, tensed and ready to react at a second's notice. He hugged the wall of the general store to make himself as oblique a target as possible.

'Show yourself, mister,' he demanded of his informant.

The response to his demand was the blinding flash of an exploding pistol. Benteen felt a thud in his chest, followed by a searing pain which was thankfully brief. In fact, to escape the awful sensation of his heart being ripped apart, the marshal gladly gave himself over to the pain-free darkness of the pit he was tumbling headlong into.

Sam Benteen's killer knew that he had only seconds to complete the task set him by Spence Barrett to earn the thousand dollars bulging in his trouser pocket. He took a rock and rubbed it hard against Dan's left shoulder until the wound was raw and bleeding, then he threw the rock into the darkness. He then fired a shot in the air from Benteen's gun. He had already shot the marshal with Tallow's gun. Now both guns had been used and the illusion he wanted to create was, hopefully, completed.

The idea behind his preparations was that folk would assume that Benteen had fired first and had wounded Tallow, but had left him able to return fire and kill the marshal. Scene set, he ran to the opening of the alley and began hollering excitedly as windows along Main lit up and folk, some in nightclothes, appeared.

On cue, Spence Barrett and his cohorts were piling out of the Tipperary Shamrock.

'Hey, everyone!' Benteen's killer shouted. 'That troublemaker, Tallow, has murdered the US marshal in cold blood. I seen him do it.'

Sheriff Lou Metzler had been anxiously waiting in his office for his entrance to the treachery being enacted, and now rushed from the law office. In no time at all the alley was full of curious and very angry citizens. There was no shortage of willing hands to help Metzler haul a groggy Dan Tallow to his feet. And equally no lack of witnesses to Tallow's bad-tempered departure from the saloon.

'You were on the wrong end of his temper your-self tonight, Lou,' Barrett reminded Metzler.

'Sure was, folks,' Metzler told the crowd. 'Thought that Tallow was going to kill me when I tried to break up a card game in the saloon.'

'Hang the bastard right now!' another player in Spence Barrett's employ called out, rousing the crowd's ire to a frenzy.

'Hold on,' Metzler announced, as the crowd pressed in on Dan, 'Tallow will hang all right. But he's murdered a man who devoted his life to upholding the law. And that's what Sam Benteen would want us to do now. I'll telegraph for a judge, and twelve good men will deliver their verdict. That's the way Marshal Benteen would have wanted it. Tallow will be hanged by the law that Sam Benteen so honestly and zealously upheld. Now, you good folk go back to bed.'

Lou Metzler grabbed Dan and hauled him along with him to the jail. Tallow, still befuddled by the Mexican's potion-laced whiskey, offered little resistance, and in fact welcomed the cell cot on to which Lou Metzler pitched him.

In the alley, Spence Barrett enlisted the help of a crony to help him take Sam Benteen's body to the undertaker's, making an outward show of deepest sympathy, while all the time laughing inside. Mame Rockton would be pleased, and when Mame Rockton was pleased she could be a very generous woman in cash and kind.

His night's play-acting over, Barrett rode out of town to report to his boss.

Mame Rockton listened with increasing pleasure to her foreman's report of the night's events
in town.

'A fine night's work, Spence,' was her view.
'Benteen's dead, and Tallow's done for.'

She went to the wall safe, took out a wad of
dollar bills and handed them over to Barrett, who
was deeply appreciative of their bulky feel. Then
Mame poured him a generous whiskey, but
warned, 'Don't you fall asleep on me now, Spence.'
She took his hand and drew him out of the room
to the stairs. 'I want you wide awake, alive and kicking!'

Leading Barrett upstairs to her bedroom, Mame
paused to check on Beth Rockton to make sure
she was asleep.

'That damn kid wanders about all over the
house,' she said. 'Wouldn't want her walking in on
me and you, Spence. Not with what I've got in
mind.'

Spence Barrett waited in the hall while Mame
went to check on Beth, the blood surging in his
veins at the prospect of the long and pleasure-
filled night ahead. The shriek that came from Beth
Rockton's room rocked Barrett out of his reverie.

Bursting out the bedroom, Mame Rockton
declared: 'Beth's gone!'

CHAPTER FIFTEEN

Reb Johnson went to the window for the hundredth time to look out. She had enjoyed the meal with Hymie Goldberg, with him regaling her about his exploits of trying to court Beth Rockton, stories which often bordered on the hilarious.

'Some day Beth and me are going to leave this place,' he had said, his dark eyes shining with hope. 'That you can count on, Mrs Johnson.'

She had been on the verge of telling Hymie to call her Reb, but had held her tongue. It was not the done thing for a youngster such as Hymie Goldberg to be on first-name terms with a woman twice his age, and a widow, too.

'Dan'll be fine, Mrs Johnson,' Hymie reassured Reb. 'That *hombre* is as tough as rawhide. Well able to take care of himself.'

'Spence Barrett is a snake, Hymie,' Reb fretted. 'And the thing about snakes is that it's usually too late to avoid being bitten when you find that they're lurking.' Then, a touch impatiently, she chided Hymie: 'Why did you let Dan go to town anyway, Hymie? And him not knowing the nest of vipers he was walking into.'

'Stop him?' Hymie blurted. 'I'd have had to shoot him to do that.'

Miserably, Reb Johnson flung back: 'At least he'd have been shot by a friend.'

The argument might have become more heated but for the sound of an approaching rider. Hymie sprang from his chair at the table to join Reb at the window, both of them jostling to see who the rider was. On seeing Beth Rockton, Reb Johnson's heart sank, while Hymie Goldberg's near leaped out of his mouth. He yanked open the door and ran across the yard to greet Beth, pulling her from her saddle into his arms.

When his elation at seeing her dipped, he asked angrily: 'Beth, what in tarnation do you think you're doing, riding round in this country on your own at night?'

'It's Mr Tallow, Hymie . . .'

Hymie's concern was instant. 'Dan? What about him, Beth?'

'He's in danger, Hymie. Terrible danger.'

'I knew it. Spence Barrett's scheming, right?'

Beth Rockton's shoulders slumped. 'Him and

my stepma. I overheard them plotting Mr Tallow's misfortune. I called to the Lowry farm to warn him, but you weren't there. Then I decided to go to town to tell Sheriff Metzler—'

'Metzler!' Hymie groaned. 'Metzler's in your stepma's pay, and as twisted as a sliding snake, Beth.'

'I figured that might be so, Hymie. That's why I came here to talk to Mrs Johnson, to ask her what I should do.'

Hymie hugged Beth to him.

'And I'm sure glad that you did, Beth. Because if Barrett and your stepma've been planning trouble for Dan, you can be certain that Lou Metzler is up to his neck and more.'

Reb, who had immediately come from the house to follow Hymie, was beside herself with worry. Hymie was heading for his horse.

'You stay put with Mrs Johnson, Beth,' he ordered, adding manfully, 'and don't you ladies fret none.'

'You're going to town, Hymie,' Beth wailed, clutching him to her. 'That's crazy.'

Hymie Goldberg, maturing years in seconds, held Beth Rockton at arm's length. 'I owe my life to Dan Tallow, Beth. Now is the time to pay back my debt.'

'Your life?' Beth questioned.

'My life,' Hymie confirmed.

He had opened a can of worms, and there was

119

no way out now but to tell Beth how Dan Tallow had done that.

Beth was aghast. 'Tried to hang you? Because of me?'

'That, and being a Jew, Beth. I'm not sure which reason was uppermost in Spence Barrett's mind, but hanged, it wouldn't matter to me none.'

Hymie mounted up and galloped off.

'Oh, Mrs Johnson,' Beth fretted. 'What will I do if anything happens to Hymie? I love him so.'

Reb Johnson put an arm around Beth Rockton and guided her to the house, staunchly reassuring her. 'Hymie will be just fine, Beth. Dan Tallow, too.'

Reb's words were fighting words, but her heart was heavy. The previous night, when Dan had left to join Hymie in the barn, she had bemoaned her lack of courage for not keeping him with her. Dan Tallow was not perfect, but then what man was? However, she reckoned that his finer qualities, given a chance to shine, would far outweigh his faults. She was not thinking of him yet as Jack Johnson's replacement, but Reb knew that if another man ever stepped into her late husband's shoes, it would be Dan Tallow.

As the Apache potion wore off, Tallow's world was spinning back in to place. He had a godalmighty headache, and how had he injured his left shoulder?

'Sheriff Metzler,' Dan called out, to get answers to his questions.

He had been playing cards. And as far as he knew, that was not a crime. So why was he in jail?

CHAPTER SIXTEEN

The door leading from the law office to the jail opened. Metzler filled it.

'What d'ya want, Tallow?' he growled.

Rankled by the lawman's aggressive attitude, for which he saw no good reason, Tallow flung back: 'The answer as to why you locked me up. That's what I want, Sheriff.'

'You can't be that dumb.'

'Pretend that I am, Metzler,' Dan said sourly.

Disinterested in Dan's plight, the sheriff announced to his utter shock: 'You're a stinkin' murderer, Tallow.'

'Murderer?' Dan gasped.

'That's right,' Metzler confirmed.

'Who am I supposed to have murdered?'

'No supposin' 'bout it. You shot Marshal Sam Benteen in cold blood.'

'I never heard of Sam Benteen,' Tallow complained.

'We've got a witness.'

'Then he's a liar!'

Lou Metzler shook his head. 'You're gallows bound for sure, fella.'

'Why would I do a thing like that?' Tallow questioned.

'You were liquored out of your skull, and itching for a fight.'

'I can hold my liquor,' Tallow attested.

Metzler sniggered. 'Not tonight, you couldn't. Wanted to draw on me, too. Would have, only for Spence Barrett stepping in to whack you with his gun-butt.'

That explained his headache.

'Witness, you say?' Dan quizzed Metzler.

'Sure.'

'Who?'

'Fella by the name of Nat Jones. An honest citizen,' Metzler lied. 'Nat says that he saw you lurkin' in the alley 'longside the general store as Benteen drew near. Then he says that you pulled the marshal into the alley and gunned him down without mercy.'

'I never killed a man in my life, other than in the war or in self-defence,' Dan protested.

'First time for everythin', I guess,' Lou Metzler said lazily.

The door to the jail slammed shut. And no matter how many times Dan hollered, the sheriff ignored his every shout. Befuddled, he sat on the cell cot and tried to focus his mind on the previous night. His memory was blank. Then he recalled Spence Barrett pouring him a whiskey. And after that he was looking into a black void.

'Barrett must have doctored the damn whiskey!' he concluded angrily.

CHAPTER SEVENTEEN

Hymie Goldberg drew rein on the outskirts of town and hitched his horse to a tree. He unsheathed his rifle and made his way forward on foot, his eyes searching the shadows, ready to react as best he could if one of the shifting shadows became solid and menacing. He could hear the distant and unusually muted sounds coming from the Tipperary Shamrock saloon. Lou Metzler, he'd know the sheriff's lumbering gait anywhere, was hanging around outside the saloon, like an actor waiting in the wings for his cue. Obviously having got his cue, Metzler then stepped inside.

An argument was breaking out. Hymie recognized the strident voice as Dan Tallow's.

He hurried along the boardwalk and edged up to the saloon window. What Hymie saw puzzled and surprised him. Dan Tallow was skunk drunk and challenging Metzler. He was faced with a dilemma. If he stepped into the saloon, his lack of gun prowess, if trouble flared, would be a drawback. He couldn't expect to be as lucky as he had been in his previous encounter with the Rockton hardmen. However, if he did not intervene, it looked like Dan Tallow would become one of two things: dead, or a killer.

He did not know how fast Dan was with a sixgun. But he did know how fast Lou Metzler was, and that was pretty fast.

Hymie, sweat running off him like water, made a decision. He was about to enter the saloon when Spence Barrett took charge and clipped Tallow on the side of the head with his gun. Tallow dropped. Then he was hauled to the door and tossed out in to the street. Hymie sank back into the shadows as Spence Barrett put in a brief appearance. As it turned out, precious seconds were lost.

Ranting and raving like a wild animal, Dan Tallow picked himself up and wandered off along the street. Passing an alley near the general store, he seemed to stumble into the alley. Smugly satisfied, Barrett went back inside the saloon, crossing paths with Metzler as he hurried out.

Hymie Goldberg was about to follow Dan to see to his safety, when another figure came from the hotel. After a brief check of the street, the man made quick tracks for the alley into which Tallow had stumbled. Passing close to Hymie, standing

126

stock-still in the shadows near the saloon, he could see the star of a US marshal on the man's shirt, and his heart skipped a beat. This was the man that Mame Rockton and Spence Barrett had hatched a plan to kill, and to have Dan Tallow hanged for his murder.

In hindsight, a couple of minutes later, Hymie regretted his indecision in not stepping out of the shadows to warn Sam Benteen of the Rockton plot. But, confused and uncertain, he had delayed. Of course, he consoled himself shortly after, he could not have predicted the swift passage of murder which was to be enacted.

Benteen was at the corner of the general store, calling into the alley for what must have been a prearranged meeting. An indistinct voice answered back, and the US marshal entered the alley. Suddenly, in the startling way that pending danger sharpens a man's instincts, Hymie Goldberg knew what was about to happen. A shout of warning was on his lips, but the blast of a gun stilled his tongue. It was too late for warnings. A few seconds later a second shot was fired. Then, a short spell after that, a man came running from the alley, hollering that murder had been committed by Dan Tallow.

Mame Rockton's scheme had worked to perfection.

Events now moved swiftly. An angry mob gathered, calling for Dan to be strung up. Metzler, to

Hymie's dismay, resisted their call and gave a speech about what Sam Benteen would have wanted. He hauled Dan off to jail to await trial. There was nothing he could do. In the confusion, Hymie slipped out of town and made tracks for Reb Johnson's, hoping that Metzler would continue to ignore the calls for Dan's lynching. Barrett and his cronies were hanging around, and anything could happen. But a lynching would bring another US marshal calling, which would defeat the whole purpose of framing Dan Tallow. Hymie was sure that the plan would call for Dan to be tried by a judge and jury and be legally but wrongly hanged.

'Damn, Dan,' Hymie swore angrily, as he galloped towards Reb Johnson's. 'Why didn't you listen when I told you that Spence Barrett was up to no good?'

Reb Johnson came running to meet Hymie Goldberg as he thundered into the yard, leaping from leather long before his horse came to a standstill.

'Trouble?' Reb asked anxiously, knowing what the answer would be.

'Heaps of trouble, Mrs Johnson,' Hymie confirmed. 'Dan's got a date with the hangman.'

Even in the darkness of the night, Hymie Goldberg could see the colour drain from Reb Johnson's face, and he was just in time to grab her as her legs folded under her. He helped her to the house. Beth, asleep in a chair by the fire, had been roused from sleep by Hymie's frantic arrival and now greeted him sleepily as he helped Reb Johnson inside the house.

'Brew some coffee, Beth,' Hymie said. 'Hot and strong.' He seated Reb in the chair vacated by Beth, where she sat as limp as a damp fuse, staring bleakly into the fire's dancing flames. 'Dan will be OK,' Hymie reassured her.

But when she looked at him, there was no belief in her eyes that that would be so.

Beth returned with the coffee.

'Wait,' Hymie said, and went to rummage in a press. He returned with a bottle of rye, from which Dan Tallow had had a generous helping the previous night. He liberally laced the coffee and handed it to Reb. While she sipped disconsolately at the coffee, Hymie paced the floor, desperately trying to figure out a way to extricate Tallow from the bind he was in. The last thing he had expected was for Reb Johnson to fold the way she had. She was normally a strong-willed, determined and resourceful woman. But Hymie supposed that her love for Dan, for he was certain now by her reaction to his predicament that Reb Johnson had fallen for Tallow, had robbed her of those attributes, floundering as she was in a sea of misery.

'I've got an idea, Hymie,' Beth Rockton said

quietly, as if unsure as to whether she should state her plan or not.

'If you've got one, say it, Beth,' Hymie urged. 'I need all the help I can get, and as fast as I can get it.'

Hymie carefully listened to Beth's plan to rally the local farmers and small ranchers in the valley to help Dan Tallow. Hymie was not wholly convinced that Beth's plan would work, giving as a reason: 'They'll not want to clash with your stepma, Beth.'

'They're all under her thumb, Hymie,' Beth reasoned. 'Maybe they'll see this as a chance to change the way things are done in the valley.'

'Maybe,' Hymie agreed. He took Beth's hands in his. 'Ain't you afraid of what all this will do to your stepma, Beth?'

Tears welled up in Beth Rockton's blue eyes. 'Sure I am, Hymie. For my dead pa's sake. But I can't just ignore what's happened.'

'When all this is over and done with, will you come away with me, Beth?' Hymie asked, his heart stilled until she answered:

'Yes, Hymie. I will.'

Even Hymie Goldberg's yelp of delight did not shake Reb Johnson from the dark world into which she had sunk.

'Before we try and band the ranchers and farmers together, Beth, I think *we* should face up to your stepma first,' Hymie said.

130

'No, Hymie,' Beth pleaded. 'She'll have you shot on sight. And if she doesn't shoot you, Spence Barrett will hang you.'

Resolved, Hymie said: 'We'll do this right, Beth. We'll give your stepma every chance to say what she's got to say, and do what she's got to do. If she wants to.'

'Oh, Hymie,' Beth wailed.

CHAPTER EIGHTEEN

It was a smug Lou Metzler who shoved Dan's food tray under the cell door.

'Eat hearty, Tallow,' he said. ''Cause you won't have many meals left to eat. As good fortune would have it, Judge Josiah Harvey is holding court in Pander. That's a town only twenty miles south of here. He's on his way here. Harvey likes a good hanging. I reckon that shortly after the judge holds court, you'll swing for Sam Benteen's murder.'

'I'm an innocent man and you know it, Metzler,' Tallow argued. 'That whole blackjack game in the saloon last night was a set-up to get me in to town and railroad me for Benteen's murder. The whiskey Spence Barrett gave me was spiked.'

'Yeah?' Metzler drawled scoffingly.

'I figure that some kind of potion was added to the whiskey. The kind of crazy juice that the

Apaches concoct. I've seen men go clear loco on Indian brew.'

Metzler looked at Dan Tallow with wry amusement. 'You don't say? Apache crazy juice, huh?' His tone was even more derisory.

'Their medicine men have old secrets about what can be got from roots and plants. Good and bad. There was a Mex hanging round last night, a half-breed. He'd know how to drive a man loco. And I figure that he was a crony of Spence Barrett.'

'A Mex, you say?' Lou Metzler shrugged. 'I saw no Mexican.'

'You're a downright liar!' Tallow barked.

'Hey, hold on now,' the sheriff protested. 'Callin' a man a liar gives him the right to protect his good name, Tallow.'

Dan Tallow said: 'We can step outside if you want, Metzler.'

Lou Metzler sneered. 'You'd like that, wouldn't you? Give you a chance to hit the trail to nowhere. Well, that ain't goin' to happen, mister. Hangin' you will be my satisfaction and pleasure.' The sheriff's grin was the smug sneer of a man who reckoned he had all eventualities covered. 'You know, that's a real interestin' tall-tale you tell, Tallow. Why don't you tell it to Judge Harvey?' He strolled to the door leading back into the law office. 'He won't believe tiddly of it. But the laughter will sure lighten up the proceedin's.'

'I'm not going to hang for something I didn't

do, Metzler,' Dan Tallow growled. 'You know I'm innocent. You're part of this whole rotten scheme, and when this is over, I'll come looking for you to settle accounts.'

There was a flash of doubt and fear in the crooked lawman's eyes, but it held for as long as a puff of smoke in a gale.

'You ain't going nowhere, 'cept to a gallows, Tallow,' he snarled.

'You'd better pray that that will be so, Metzler. Or you'll be wormbait!'

Lou Metzler's Adam's apple bobbed. 'Hah!' he grunted, and slammed the door shut.

Dan Tallow languished disconsolately on the cell bunk, his gut heaving at the sight of the greasy *mélange* that passed as food. He could huff and puff all he liked, but the jail was not going to fall down. On hearing the sound of shuffling feet and sniggering in the alley outside, he looked up at the cell window to see a dangling hangman's noose. He charged angrily to the window, but the scatter of running feet told him that his taunters would be long gone.

Tallow had his regrets, because there were many things, given the chance, which he would have done differently. But his biggest regret of all was that if he was hanged, he would miss a lot of years in Reb Johnson's company. Of course he could not be sure that she would fall in love with him, but there were signs that had given him hope; a hope he could now abandon.

At the other side of the door leading to the cells, Lou Metzler's scoffing leave of Dan Tallow quickly turned to a shaky fear. What if something went wrong and Tallow cheated the hangman? Or maybe he'd find some way of busting out of jail? Unlikely on both counts, was Metzler's verdict, once he got control over his nerves. But no matter how he tried, he was still haunted by the thought that, by some cruel twist of fate, he would have to face Dan Tallow. He knew from his confrontation with Tallow in the Tipperary Shamrock that he had a fast draw. And he knew that until Tallow was swinging in the breeze at the end of a rope, he had good cause to worry.

Lou Metzler was resigned to sweating a lot until the gallows trapdoor opened and Tallow dropped through it.

Much to Hymie Goldberg's relief, morning saw a return of Reb Johnson's feistiness. She had shed her tears and was now in fighting mood. Fetching a rifle, she said: 'We've got no-goods to flush out, Hymie!'

'Yes, ma'am,' he said, trailing her to the door.

'Riders coming!'

Mame Rockton, devouring an enormous breakfast, lost her appetite at the ranch hand's announcement.

'How many, Sullivan?' she asked.

'Three. A distance off yet, but it looks like the Widder Johnson, Hymie Goldberg and Miss Rockton, ma'am.'

Mame Rockton swept her plate from the table. 'So, *that's* where the brat got to!'

The rancher had not lost any sleep about her stepdaughter's disappearance the night before. In fact, she had hoped that she had seen the last of her. Since Mame had come to the ranch as Abe Rockton's second wife, Beth Rockton had not accepted her presence as much as her lily-livered father had pleaded with her to.

Mame Rockton had despised her husband, and had married him only for the ease and comfort of life as a rancher's wife. From early on she had found her pleasures outside of the marriage bed, with Spence Barrett and Rico Suarez. She was a woman who liked dangerous men, and Abe Rockton was too kindly a gentleman for her liking. Of course, he was not blind or deaf, and soon suspected his wife's wandering ways. When he walked in on Barrett and Mame in the barn, he had gone straight back to the house and shot himself. Mame put out the story that it was a gun-cleaning accident. Lou Metzler had not challenged her story, and no one else had dared do so.

Leaving, his back to the rancher, Sullivan's face had a look of utter contempt. Most of the men who had worked for Abe Rockton despised his second wife. Decent and hard-working men, they saw Beth Rockton as the real owner of the Rockton ranch, and disagreed profoundly with Mame Rockton's skullduggery and her employment of hardcases such as Spence Barrett and Rico Suarez against her husband's wishes.

No one could understand why Abe Rockton, a decent man, had married Mame Bradley, a slut. The opinion was that he must have had some kind of brain seizure that scattered his good sense for long enough to allow Mame to hook him.

The punchers hanging around outside the house were uneasy and fretful as Reb Johnson led Hymie and Beth in to the yard, closely watched by a sullen-faced Spence Barrett and the cruelly featured Mexican, Suarez.

'What're you doing here?' Barrett barked at Reb Johnson. 'You're not welcome.'

'Yes, she is,' Beth Rockton piped up. 'Hymie, too.'

Barrett snorted. 'You shouldn't be hangin' around with rats and Jews, Miss Rockton. Not that there's any difference in my book.'

Beth Rockton's face flushed with anger. Her gaze on Barrett and Suarez was unwavering. 'If there are any rats around here, I'm looking at them.'

Putting in a stormy appearance, Mame Rockton demanded to know: 'Where have you been all night, young woman?'

'With Reb Johnson, and,' she emphasized, 'Hymie. And a night under the same roof as decent folk was surely a welcome change.'

'Get in the house,' her stepmother ordered. 'I'll deal with you later.'

'No,' Beth refused defiantly.

'Get in the house, you brat!' Mame yelled.

'If it's all right with you, Mrs Johnson,' Beth said, 'I'd like to stay a spell.'

'Fine with me, Beth,' Reb replied.

'Want me to get Miss Rockton inside the house, ma'am?' Spence Barrett asked, starting towards Beth.

'You touch me, Barrett,' Beth said in a cold rage, 'and I'll kill you.'

'And if Beth doesn't, I will,' Hymie Goldberg promised.

Barrett laughed derisively and kept coming.

'And if they don't, *I* will.'

Reb Johnson levelled her rifle on the Rockton foreman. Spence Barrett's steps faltered.

Mame Rockton said, 'Spence asked you a question which you did not answer. What're you doing here, if it's not to deliver Beth back safely?'

'I've . . .' Reb Johnson's gaze took in her unlikely partners and she amended: 'No, *we've* come here to demand that you admit to the skullduggery which has put Dan Tallow unjustly in jail and facing a noose.'

'Demand, *señora?*' Rico Suarez stepped forward.

138

'Demand is a big word, when all you've got for backup is a girl and a boy. This is fast gun range, *señora*. You're out of your depth.'

The tense reaction of the crew to the Mexican's menacing intervention worried Mame Rockton. A slight shift of her eyes was the signal for Spence Barrett to rail in Suarez.

'Why don't you see to that chore I gave you to do, Rico?' Barrett said.

For a hair-raising second, Barrett sweated that the Mexican's smouldering resentment would backlash on him, but he stalked off.

Reb Johnson swung her horse about. 'We're wasting our time here, talking to the devil's sister,' she told Beth and Hymie. 'Let's head straight to town. I reckon that it's time to wire the territorial capital to send another marshal.' She briefly drew rein to address her parting remarks to the ranch boss. 'I figure that Lou Metzler is up to his eyeballs in Dan Tallow's downfall. I also think that he'll squirm and spill his guts when the next US marshal rides into town.'

Mame Rockton maintained her pose of casual indifference to Reb Johnson's threat. But under her feet she felt the ground shift, and she worried that the shift might be the prelude to a great yawning chasm opening up.

CHAPTER NINETEEN

Lou Metzler, pondering on Dan Tallow's threat to even the score if he got free of his bind, gave the sheriff more and more nerves. A coward, he did not fancy leaving even the slightest chance of Tallow making good on his threat. A day was not long to have to wait to hang his prisoner, but Metzler's nerves were so raw that even that short time seemed an age. So he figured that he would solve his dilemma there and then. He would fall back on a ruse he had used a couple of times before to rid Mame Rockton of thorny problems. He could see no reason why the same trick should not work again.

'Like to stretch those long legs of yours, Tallow?' he invited, pleasantly.

The sheriff's generous gesture took Dan Tallow by surprise. And it might have worked, too, had Tallow not already been burned by ignoring Hymie Goldberg's good advice. He knew that

Hymie thought as little of Lou Metzler as he did of Spence Barrett. But he'd play along, and see what treachery Metzler had in mind. Whatever connivery the rotten lawman was up to, might also backfire on him and give Tallow the chance to escape to try and clear his name. Though Dan did not hold out much chance of that in a town bought and paid for by Mame Rockton.

'That cell is pretty cramped,' Metzler said.

'Yeah, it sure is,' Tallow agreed.

The sheriff unlocked the cell door and stepped back, gun in hand. 'Don't want to take any chances,' he said.

'Makes sense,' Tallow replied. 'When you say, stretch my legs: does that mean outside?'

Metzler shook his head. 'Uh-uh. Someone might take a potshot at you. Just round the office a coupla times should do just fine.'

Tallow did not like the idea of the sheriff behind him with a cocked gun, but if he stayed locked in his cell there would be no chance at all to make a getaway. So it was all a matter of balancing risks, he decided.

'You're the bossman,' Tallow said, and strolled around.

Luck favoured Dan. In the shaving-mirror on the wall to the right of the door, he caught sight of Lou Metzler his gun drawing a bead on him, a killing lust brightening his narrow eyes to the intensity of a diamond. So, *that* was the plan. Just when he'd reach the door, the sheriff would shoot him in the back, as if he had been attempting to escape. No one would dare question the cock-and-bull story he would proffer as evidence of Tallow's break for freedom.

Tallow ducked. Metzler's bullet ripped a chunk from the door. Dan spun round and leaped through the air to close the gap between him and the sheriff, before he had time to get off another round. He crashed down on the lawman, just as he pointed his .45. Dan expected to feel the burn and pain of a bullet slicing through his gut, but fortune favoured him, and as Metzler fell backwards the gun turned his way just as he squeezed the trigger. A gaping hole appeared in the sheriff's chest. Blood spurted from the ragged wound. He gasped one breath, and that was all his shattered lungs could manage.

Tallow knew that he had to act quickly. There was no time to hang around to explain what had happened. No one would believe him. And no one would wait for Judge Josiah Harvey to render a verdict of guilty, as doubly inevitable as that now was.

Feet were running along the boardwalk. An excited woman's voice was raised.

'The shot came from the jail!'

With time running out faster than a politician's election promises, all Tallow was able to do was grab Metzler's pistol and dash for the door. On opening it, he saw angry faces closing in on him from all sides. Suddenly the crowd eased their rush to the law office, and Tallow realized that the gun he was holding was not the primary deterrent – horror was. He looked down at himself and saw the sheriff's blood on his shirt and trousers, and on his hands, too.

'Someone get a damn rope!' a man's voice called out.

Arriving on the edge of town to see its citizens rushing along Main to the jail, Reb Johnson asked one of the excited men: 'What seems to be the problem, Jed?'

'That fella Tallow's just cut down Lou Metzler in cold blood, Reb.'

The blood drained from Reb Johnson's face.

'Dan is no cold-blooded killer, Mrs Johnson,' Hymie Goldberg cried. 'He's no killer, cold-blooded or otherwise!'

With Reb Johnson in a stunned daze, it was left to Hymie to take her reins and lead her to the jail. And then, seeing the blood on Dan Tallow's clothes and the wild look in his eyes, even Hymie Goldberg's faith was shaken.

CHAPTER TWENTY

Tallow's explanation of what had taken place was pitched directly to Reb Johnson and Hymie Goldberg.

'You expect us to believe that?' a man whom Hymie recognized as a Rockton man derided. 'Unlike you, Tallow, Lou Metzler was no sneak killer.' He turned to the swelling crowd. 'I say we do the right thing and string this bastard up right now.'

A more moderate voice argued for the arrival of Judge Josiah Harvey, reasoning, 'Harvey's a hanging judge anyway.'

Hymie saw the Rockton man glance another man's way, who slid into a nearby alley. His direction, Hymie figured, would take him to the rear of the jail and through its back door to come up on Dan Tallow from behind.

Hymie shouted a warning: 'There's a man gone round back, Dan!'

No sooner had Hymie shouted his warning than the man burst through the door from the cells, pistol at the ready. Tallow swung around in a low crouch and fired. The man screamed as his kneecap shattered. His cohort outside the jail urged the crowd forward. Hymie leaped from leather and on to the boardwalk to stand alongside Dan, his rifle cocked. The Rockton man stopped dead in his tracks. He had heard about Hymie Goldberg's shooting skills when Dan Tallow had made his first visit to town and had tangled with Spence Barrett. He did not know that, on that occasion, Hymie's so-called expertise with a rifle was nothing but pure luck.

'I'll plug the first man who moves!' Hymie cautioned.

'He's bluffin',' the Rockton hand snorted.

'You figure, Ned?' a man near him said. 'Then you charge the jail first.'

'Reb,' Hymie called out, 'I need you to back my play here.'

Reb Johnson pulled herself together and covered the crowd with her rifle, holding the crowd under a threat of crossfire.

Dan Tallow said: 'Reb, I swear to you that I did not kill the US marshal or Metzler. I was set up.'

'I know you were set up for the US marshal's

murder, Dan,' Reb said. 'Tell the good people what you overheard Spence Barrett and your stepmother plotting, Beth.'

Beth Rockton told her story.

Reb Johnson said, 'Lou Metzler was as rotten as they come, and you all know that. I figure that Dan Tallow would not be the first man he shot in the back, while pretending that he was escaping.'

The Rockton man tried his best to keep the crowd from drifting away, but they slowly did. The thunder of horses arriving in town had the crowd congregating once more, as Spence Barrrett and a bevy of hardcases put in an appearance. Seeing Tallow free as a bird, and sensing the town's mood, Barrett guessed that events had swung against him and Mame Rockton.

Seeing that Tallow's fortunes had changed dramatically, the Rockton ramrod drew his rifle from its saddle scabbard and cut loose, sending a volley of shots Dan's way which tore chunks of wood from the law office door and shattered a window. Tallow was quick to second-guess Barrett and had dived to the ground, pulling Reb Johnson down with him. Hymie, whose wits in the confusion had not been quick enough, caught a bullet in the shoulder.

Tallow returned Barrett's fire, and two riders alongside him dropped. Reb Johnson felled a third. The Rockton troublestirrer of moments before, taking a sneaky advantage of Tallow's and

Reb Johnson's concentration on Barrett and his cronies, lined Dan up in his gunsights. Hymie, pale and shocked, could not do much, but he did manage to shoot at the Rockton man. He missed by a mile, but Tallow's would-be assassin had been distracted, and he paid the price of a bullet in the gut from Dan's exploding .45.

The two remaining men with Spence Barrett hightailed it. He shot one of the men in the back. The second man fired, but instead of Spence Barrett getting his lead, he blasted a late Rockton arrival out of his saddle.

When the Rockton ramrod again turned his attention to Dan Tallow, he was looking down the barrel of Dan's pistol.

'I think,' Tallow said, with deadly menace, 'that it's time we paid a visit to your boss, Barrett.' Addressing Beth Rockton, he said, 'You think that you could hold Hymie's hand while the doc fixes up that busted shoulder of his, young lady?'

Grinning from ear to ear, Beth said, her blue eyes dreamy: 'Nothing I'd like better, Mr Tallow.'

'I don't need no nursing,' Hymie Goldberg protested. 'I'm a man.'

'I guess you are at that, Hymie,' Dan Tallow said. 'But what man wouldn't want a pretty lady holding his hand?'

Hymie chuckled. 'You know, Dan,' he said, 'you might just have a point there.'

'I'll be back, Reb,' Dan told Reb Johnson. And turning his attention to Spence Barrett, he ordered: 'Ride!'

CHAPTER TWENTY-ONE

The ride to the Rockton ranch was an edgy trip.
Tallow knew that the slightest slip on his part, and
the crafty Spence Barrett would grab his chance to
turn the tables. And it worried Dan that once he
reached Rockton range, he would have a mighty
hard time leaving it alive.

'If you had any sense you'd turn tail, Tallow,' was
the Rockton foreman's advice. And under the
circumstances, Tallow reckoned, very sound advice
it was. 'The Rockton crew will be all over you the
second you hit Rockton land. You won't stand a
chance,' Barrett smugly predicted.

Soon after, Barrett spotted a Rockton outrider
and hollered: 'Go tell Mame Rockton that she's
got company, Andy.'

The man changed course and took off at a
gallop. Dan Tallow got the fleeing man in his

sights, but though it would have made sense to bring him down, he could not get himself to pull a trigger on an innocent man.

'That's the difference between you and me, Tallow,' Barrett taunted. 'I'd have cut him down without qualm or mercy.'

'That's a mighty big difference that I'm really glad exists between us, Barrett,' Tallow growled.

Soon other riders began to pace Tallow, obviously unsure of what they should do. That they did not intervene, Tallow figured, was down to the risk their foreman was in. But how long before a shooter sought out a sniper's position?

Surprisingly, a half-hour later, they safely reached the Rockton ranch house. Mame Rockton, alerted by the messenger, was waiting on the porch for their arrival.

'Well, Mr Tallow,' she greeted Dan. 'I thought you were crazy when you saved Hymie Goldberg's neck, but I never thought you were loco enough to come riding in here on your own. So, why have you come?'

'To haul you back to town to stand trial for your misdeeds, ma'am,' Tallow doggedly stated.

Spence Barrett laughed. 'Hey, Rico,' Dan looked to the Mexican coming from the side of the house, 'that Apache loco-weed you spiked Tallow's whiskey with must still be workin'!'

'Guess so, Spence.' The Mexican spread his legs and took up a gunfighter's stance. 'I told Señora

Johnson that this is fast gun range, Señor Tallow. How fast are you?'

'Fast enough,' Dan retorted.

'I don't think so, *señor*,' Suarez said.

'Looks like Rico is throwin' down the gauntlet to you, Tallow,' Barrett sneered. 'Are you man enough to face him?'

'And turn my back on you?' Dan snorted.

'No man shoots,' the foreman told the men drifting back into the yard. Barrett offered his hands to Tallow. 'Tie my hands if you want.'

Tallow said: 'I guess we've got a score to settle all right, Mex.'

'Don't call me Mex!' Suarez snarled.

'Don't let him get to you, Rico,' Mame Rockton advised.

'No, ma'am.'

'Keep that fiery temper of yours under control.'

'Yes, ma'am.'

Tallow wondered if he should gamble on the fight going out of Barrett and Mame Rockton if he outdrew and killed Suarez. Barrett was poison, but nothing as potent a poison as the Mexican. Suarez was the kind of devil's bastard that would terrify any man on the Rockton payroll. Having him out of the way might smooth his path some.

But was he fast enough?

Dan Tallow let out a long sigh and stepped down from his horse. If he was not fast enough, it would not matter to him one jot.

Now that his challenge had been accepted, Rico Suarez became edgy. Maybe it was a trick of the light, or Dan's hope taking flight, but he could have sworn that the half-breed had paled. Could it be that he had been bluffing?

'You call it, Mex,' Tallow said.

Hatred and anger twisted Suarez's face. His right hand dived for his gun. He was lightning-fast, but Dan Tallow's pistol cleared leather a hair's-breadth before the Mexican's. And that's all that was needed. The sound of both guns merged and rolled out across the fertile range. Rico Suarez laughed, the way a victor might. Spence Barrett and Mame Rockton, who had been stunned by Tallow's speed, had their spirits lifted, but only for the briefest second until the Mexican wobbled and fell backwards. Barrett, true to form, kicked out at Tallow, catching him with a boot on the side of the head. Dan's fall was a heavy one, and his gun spun out of his hand and, more importantly, out of his reach. Barrett jumped clear of his horse and grabbed the pistol. Standing over Tallow, he snarled:

'A bullet or a rope. The end's the same, Tallow.'

'Drop it, Barrett.' The Rockton ramrod looked to his left where Sullivan, the man who had earlier alerted Mame Rockton to the arrival of Reb Johnson, Hymie Goldberg and Beth Rockton stepped forward. 'There's been enough killing and skullduggery. It's time it stopped, and this valley got back to the good times when Abe Rockton ran things around here and folk got good neighbourliness and fair dealing. I figure it'll be like that again when this ranch is run by Beth Rockton, whose ranch it really is.'

Spence Barrett's attitude was one of contemptuous dismissal. Ben Sullivan was the best puncher that the Rockton ranch or any other outfit in the territory had, but he was no gunfighter.

'I think,' Barrett said, 'that you should attend to whatever chores you have to do, Sullivan, and leave the business of chastising Mrs Rockton's troublemakers to me.'

Barrett turned his attention back to Dan Tallow, who said: 'Give me a gun and make this a fair fight, Barrett.'

The foreman scoffed and levelled his gun on Tallow. He glanced to the house porch for Mame Rockton's approval, and got it.

'Hope you play a nice harp, Tallow,' he mocked.

Spence Barrett froze at the sound of guns being cocked. He turned his head slowly, his eyes popping at the row of men with guns drawn. A couple still had their guns holstered, but were far outnumbered by the men Ben Sullivan led.

'Like I said,' Sullivan called out, loud enough for Mame Rockton to hear, 'this ranch is rightly Beth Rockton's, and me and the boys aim to see that she gets her rightful due. Now, you folks,' his gaze took in Mame Rockton, Spence Barrett and the small coterie of men still siding with them, 'can wait for Judge Harvey to arrive. Or you can hightail it right now with just the clothes on your backs!'

Spence Barrett's cronies quickly grabbed Sullivan's offer to hit the trail. Isolated, Barrett and Mame Rockton soon followed. As they rode out of the yard, the former ramrod spun round in his saddle, sixgun spitting at Dan Tallow. Ben Sullivan slung him a rifle, and Tallow blasted Barrett out of his saddle, which hastened Mame Rockton's departure.

Judge Josiah Harvey looked with considerable displeasure at the temporary sheriff until an election could be held, and thunderously repeated the sheriff's words: 'No hanging?'

'No, Judge,' Dan Tallow said. 'All of the matters which would have resulted in a hanging, if truth and justice had not won out, have been happily resolved.'

'I can't say that I am happy with making a trip to this one-horse burg and not having a hanging by way of compensation for my efforts, Sheriff,' Josiah Harvey boomed. He stepped back a pace from Dan Tallow. 'I thought the sheriff's name was Metzler.'

'It was, Judge.'

A flicker of apprehension showed in the judge's whiskey-washed eyes. 'And Tallow was the name of the man to be hanged?'

Dan Tallow grinned. 'Right again.' Tallow took the liberty of placing an arm round Josiah Harvey's shoulders. 'It's a real long and boring story, Judge, which you might want to listen to over, ah . . . let's say some *liquid refreshment*, your honour,' Dan suggested.

Harvey licked parched lips. 'Mighty generous of you, Sheriff Tallow.'

An hour later, and with two bottles of clear glass on the table between them, Dan Tallow had all the loose ends of the previous couple of turbulent days tied up, calling witnesses as required to back his story.

Maudlin of mood, Josiah Harvey confessed, 'I was really looking forward to hanging you, Tallow.'

'You can still be of use, Judge,' Dan said. 'We've got a wedding.'

'A wedding?' Josiah Harvey repeated, stunned.

'You're a judge, ain't you? Judges marry folk.'

Josiah Harvey staggered to his feet, swaying precariously, but refusing Dan's efforts to keep him upright.

'I'm a hanging judge, sir,' he told Dan.

The next day, ragged at the edges, Judge Josiah Harvey married Hymie Goldberg and Beth Rockton. Reb Johnson, standing alongside Tallow, whispered: 'It would be a pity to waste the services of the good judge, don't you think, Dan? Might as well do two ceremonies as one.'

Josiah Harvey grabbed the top of his head and

grimaced in agony on hearing Dan Tallow's wild yell of delight.

'Are you sure that there's no one to hang, Tallow?' Harvey asked, before boarding the stage.

'No, Judge,' Tallow said. 'And I don't expect we'll be needing your services around here for a long time, if ever again. Except, of course, for weddings.'

'I've had my fill of weddings,' Josiah Harvey announced. And as the stage rolled out of town, he shouted back: 'I'm a hanging judge, dammit!'

A year later, with the help of good neighbours and no small amount of back-breaking labour by the Rockton crew loaned to Dan at convenient times by Hymie and Beth Goldberg, the Tallow farm delivered up a fine yield.

Beth Goldberg had returned land grabbed by her stepmother to its rightful owners, and had taken the Rockton ranch back within its boundaries, from where in the future it would legitimately expand by paying fair prices and just dealing.

Hymie Goldberg had made the passage from boy to man with grace and honour, as had Beth to womanhood. There was a rumour of an heir to the Rockton ranch, but in the Tallow household, such a tale had gone beyond rumour, with Reb Tallow finding it more and more difficult to tie her bootlaces without Dan's help. A task which Dan Tallow

156

was glad and proud to take on.

'A boy, Dan, I reckon,' Reb said, wincing as the baby kicked.

'That'll please the child's godmother, Ma Barley, no end,' Dan said. He added proudly: 'Me, too, Reb.' He took Reb in his arms. 'Me, too,' he said, sighing contentedly.